FEMAL

Krasnow figured he had the drop on Skye Fargo. Fargo might have a gun in his holster, but Krasnow had his gun pressed against the swanlike neck of the beautiful Russian agent Galina.

"Drop your gun belt," Krasnow commanded. As Fargo obeyed, Krasnow went on, "Dmitri was sure he had killed you."

"Everybody's entitled to one mistake," Fargo said, letting one hand drop down to where his throwing knife was concealed in his calf holster.

The moment Krasnow's eyes flicked away to check on Galina, that knife was out. With a flick of his wrist, Fargo hurled it through the air—to rip into Krasnow's gun hand.

There was only one thing louder than Krasnow's howl of pain. It was Galina's voice as she commanded Fargo, "Kill him!"

Over his head in intrigue and evil, Fargo didn't know who was more bloodthirsty—the people blazing bullets at him, or the ones handing him his pay. . . .

THE SAWDUST TRAIL

by

Jon Sharpe

A SIGNET BOOK

SIGNET
Published by the Penguin Group
Penguin Books USA Inc., 375 Hudson Street,
New York, New York 10014, U.S.A.
Penguin Books Ltd, 27 Wrights Lane,
London W8 5TZ, England
Penguin Books Australia Ltd, Ringwood,
Victoria, Australia
Penguin Books Canada Ltd, 10 Alcorn Avenue,
Toronto, Ontario, Canada M4V 3B2
Penguin Books (N.Z.) Ltd, 182-190 Wairau Road,
Auckland 10, New Zealand

Penguin Books Ltd, Registered Offices:
Harmondsworth, Middlesex, England

First published by Signet,
an imprint of Dutton Signet,
a division of Penguin Books USA Inc.

First Printing, December, 1994
10 9 8 7 6 5 4 3 2

The first chapter of this book originally appeared in *Oklahoma Ordeal*, the one hundred fifty-fifth volume in this series.

 REGISTERED TRADEMARK—MARCA REGISTRADA

Printed in Canada

The Trailsman

Beginnings . . . they bend the tree and they mark the man. Skye Fargo was born when he was eighteen. Terror was his midwife, vengeance his first cry. Killing spawned Skye Fargo, ruthless, cold-blooded murder. Out of the acrid smoke of gunpowder still hanging in the air, he rose, cried out a promise never forgotten.

The Trailsman they began to call him all across the West: searcher, scout, hunter, the man who could see where others only looked, his skills for hire but not his soul, the man who lived each day to the fullest, yet trailed each tomorrow. Skye Fargo, the Trailsman, the seeker who could take the wildness of a land and the wanting of a woman and make them his own.

Oregon, 1860,
just north of the Rogue River,
where death became an echo
of faraway places . . .

1

Skye Fargo's lake-blue eyes were narrowed, his brow furrowed, as he peered at the turning, twisting road below. The coach traveling the road was unlike any he had ever seen before, a closed, high-roofed body painted entirely black, with the driver seated high and forward. No Concord and no country brougham, not even a mud wagon. It might have been a coupe, with its low, curving door and single window, but it had none of the graceful lines of a coupe. Everything about it was heavy, wheels wider, spokes thicker, the body bulky, almost cumbersome. Yet it took the uneven, twisting road with ease. He had been following it from the high hills most of the crisp fall day, and the driver was very good, very much in control of the two-horse team. Even the horses were unfamiliar, both rich chestnuts with bulging, broad chests, yet with a tallness that gave them grace as well as power.

But the coach was not the only thing he had been watching. A little after midday he had seen the five riders appear on the high land on the other side of the road, almost across from where he rode. They began to follow the coach, staying mostly in the mountain ash and the Rocky Mountain maple. Fargo's mouth grew tight as he watched the five riders. They were out for trouble. It was not just in the furtiveness of their movements, Fargo thought to himself. He felt it inside himself, that sixth sense you developed and polished with years of experience. They had doggedly followed the coach all afternoon, and now that the day began to slide toward an end they began to move downward. The furrow slid across Skye Fargo's brow as he watched. The coach driver, intent on his driving, didn't see the five riders come down onto the road behind him. Fargo took his horse downward along a shallow slope.

Below, the five riders were gaining ground on the coach. Suddenly the driver heard the sound of hoofbeats, turned and saw his pursuers. He flicked his whip over the team and the horses surged forward, but the five pursuers had drawn their six-guns and were firing. Fargo spurred the Ovaro down the slope, his eyes on the scene unfolding before him. The driver tried to flatten himself on the seat and still keep his grip on the reins. He was somehow managing to keep control of the racing team and avoid the hail of bullets when two of the riders drew up on each side of him. Their shots caught him in a cross fire and his body turned and twisted on the seat before the reins fell from his hands and he toppled over the side of the coach.

A third rider dashed past to take hold of the cheek strap of the nearest horse, and he slowly brought the team to a halt. Fargo continued to edge the Ovaro along the lower part of the slope, staying behind a thin line of hawthorns. He watched as the five men dismounted alongside the halted coach. Two yanked the coach door open and pulled a tall, bearded man wearing a long coat with a fur collar from inside. He was apparently the only passenger in the coach. He tried to fight back but was slammed to the ground. Fargo moved the Ovaro closer, still behind the tall hawthorns, and saw the five men tear the clothes from the bearded man—his coat first, then a waistcoat and vest. They held him down as they stripped him of his trousers, and Fargo watched them search each item of clothing before discarding it. The frown dug deeper into his brow. This was no ordinary stagecoach holdup. They were plainly searching for something. Now down to his long johns, the man was held on the ground by two of his attackers while the others threw the seats out of the coach as they searched inside the vehicle.

When they didn't find whatever it was they sought, they returned to the man and began beating him with kicks and vicious blows, all the while shouting questions. His lips a thin line, Fargo decided he had seen more than enough, and he reached down and drew the big Henry from its saddlecase as he moved the Ovaro farther downhill. He halted some twenty yards from the men, behind a thick shadbush just tall enough to screen him. He brought the rifle to his shoulder and fired, aiming his shot to slam into the ground beside the feet of a burly man who seemed to be the leader.

"That's enough," he called out as the bullet threw up a spray of dirt. "Get away from him."

The burly man straightened, surprise flooding his face as his eyes swept the hillside in the dusk. Fargo fired another shot into the same spot and it threw up another spray of dirt. "Sure thing, mister," the man said and backed away from the beaten figure on the ground. The others followed his lead and backed away. The burly man peered up into the trees. "Come out where we can see you," he said. "We're not looking for trouble."

"You've a strange idea of being friendly," Fargo said, and his eyes swept the five men. They were ordinary enough in looks, the kind who could be hired most anywhere to do most anything. "Drop your guns," Fargo ordered. The burly one threw a quick glance at the others and they spun as one, drawing their revolvers as they did, and sent a hail of bullets into the shadbush. Fargo dropped sideways from the saddle, the rifle in his hands, and heard the bullets whistle past him, too close for comfort. He hit the ground, rolled onto his stomach, and aimed the rifle. The five men, crouched, were still spraying bullets in his direction, and he drew a bead on one, fired, and the man flew backwards as his chest erupted in a torrent of red. He shifted the gun and fired again. A second man went down with a spinning motion. The others started to dive for cover and one tried to climb into the coach. He was halfway through the doorway when Fargo's shot caught him. He pitched forward into the carriage and lay facedown with his legs dangling outside. They twitched for a moment before they lay still.

The last two had taken cover, one behind the coach and the other in a clump of aspen marked at the base by a row of ebony sedges. Fargo crawled downward on his stomach to halt behind a thin line of scrabble brush only a dozen yards from the coach. He let his eyes sweep the scene as the lavender of dusk began to deepen. The prone figure in his underwear groaned softly but lay still, and Fargo swore under his breath. He hadn't a lot of time; the day was waning quickly and the remaining two attackers were playing possum, waiting for him to make an impatient mistake. Fargo decided the figure in the tree cover would be first and he lay the rifle down and drew the big Colt .44 as he decided to make use of the trick a trapper had taught him. It depended on quickness of eye and marksmanship, and its success lay in triggering the automatic response that was part of animal and man.

He aimed the Colt at the ebony sedges, but as he pulled the trigger his eyes were peering above the bullet's trajectory. He was ready as the shot plunged into the base of the sedges, the Colt raised as he saw the flash of answering gunfire from inside the aspen. He fired two shots and heard the gasp of pain and, seconds later, the thud of a body falling to the ground. "One to go," Fargo murmured softly as he peered at the coach. Dusk was sliding into night as he inched himself forward on his stomach. Edging through the last of the brush as darkness descended, he halted, strained his ears, and heard the sound—footsteps moving quickly and lightly. He defined the form as it came around the rear of the coach, moving fast, dark against dark.

The man ran toward one of the horses, a blurry, indistinct target, and Fargo waited, his finger poised on the trigger, until the man pulled himself into the saddle. He was still for a moment but a moment was all the Trailsman needed. Fargo fired and the figure toppled soundlessly from the saddle. Waiting a moment, Fargo pushed to his feet, picked up the rifle, and trotted past the figure, under which a dark stain was already soaking into the ground. A moon rose to afford a pale light as he halted by the man they'd been beating and dropped to one knee. The man tried to sit up and gasped out in pain. "My body . . . it is broken," he said in a heavily accented voice as Fargo helped him to sit upright. "Slowly . . . slowly," he said as Fargo's hand pressed against his back. He had a strong face above the full beard, Fargo saw, a straight, prominent nose, heavy eyebrows and heavy cheekbones, an imposing face with eyes that flashed dark blue fire despite his pain.

"Your driver's dead," Fargo said, and the man groaned.

"Poor Svetlov," he said. "But I have you to thank for my life. *Spasibo, spasibo,* my friend."

"*Spasibo*? You're Russian?" Fargo frowned back.

"*Da*. Yes. You know Russian?" the man asked.

"No, but I knew an ox-cart driver who came from Russia," Fargo said. "He taught me a few words."

"I see," the man said as a shiver ran through him with a gust of sharp night wind. "*Poojalasta,* my coat," he said.

"I'd guess you have a few broken ribs at least," Fargo said as he helped the man slowly slip into his long, heavy coat.

"*Da,*" the man said as he steadied himself against the pain. "But I must go on. Others wait for me. You will be paid very well if you can take me to where I was going."

"Where's that?" Fargo questioned as he picked up the rest of the man's clothing.

"A place called Cornpipe, a road there they call Bear Trail. There is a house at the end of the road," the man said. "It will be worth your while, believe me."

"Why did those varmints attack you? What were they looking for?" Fargo questioned.

"It was a highway robbery. They were bandits," the man said, and Fargo held the smile inside himself. The answer was a lie. It had been no ordinary holdup. But his curiosity was aroused, and he never turned down the promise of good cash.

"All right. I'll give it a try," he said.

"*Khorosho.* Good. You have name, my friend?" the man asked.

"Fargo. Skye Fargo."

"Can you find this place by night, Fargo?"

"I make a living finding places. They call me the Trailsman," Fargo said.

"*Otchen khorosho.* Very good. I am Nicholas Rhesnev."

"What are you doing here, Nicholas?" Fargo asked as he put the seats back into the coach and tossed out the body.

"Visiting friends. Learning about this America of yours," Nicholas Rhesnev said as he climbed into the coach. Fargo smiled. It was another turn-aside answer. He paused as his eyes held on the small lettering in white along the curved bottom edge of the door, five words written in the Cyrillic alphabet. Suddenly he knew why the coach was not like any he'd ever seen.

"You brought this coach with you," he remarked.

"*Da,*" Nicholas Rhesnev said, pain in his voice. "A fine vehicle, made by Bulgannin in St. Petersburg, one of our best coachmakers. I felt Svetlov could make better time driving a coach he was familiar with."

Fargo's glance went to the tall, powerful pair of chestnuts. "The horses, too," he said.

"*Da*. They are what we call Dons, bred in the steppes of Siberia," the bearded man said. "But please, let us go. The pain is too much."

Fargo whistled and the Ovaro came at once as he climbed onto the driver's seat of the coach. The pinto would trot alongside, he knew, and he snapped the reins over the team. The coach began to roll and he cast a passing glance at the bodies of the five attackers. All ordinary looking, he concluded again. He'd find nothing by searching them. "I take it you don't want to bury your driver," he called back toward the coach, leaning sideways from the seat.

"There isn't time," Rhesnev's voice returned, still full of pain, and Fargo sent the team forward faster. The horses responded quickly and handled beautifully and he settled down to his driving under the moon that slid across the sky. He had never visited Cornpipe but he knew it lay close against the western edge of the Umpqua forest, and he kept the horses driving northeast. The road stayed in mountain country. As he drove he heard an occasional moan of pain from the closed coach behind him. The bearded man's story about visiting friends in America was belied by the very coach he was driving, Fargo frowned in thought. One didn't bring over a coach, horses, and a driver for a leisurely visit to friends. Nicholas Rhesnev had wanted his arrival to be kept secret. He wanted to avoid the talk that would accompany a foreigner buying a coach and team. But the plan hadn't succeeded. The attack had proven that. Why was secrecy so important? Fargo mused as he drove northward, moving into lower ground. The Russian team, the Don horses, were still responsive and showed no signs of tiring, he noted with admiration.

The moon was past the midnight sky and he was traveling a wider road with rolling hills of canyon oak and quaking aspen on either side. The high moon afforded more of its pale light, and as normal as breathing to him, Fargo's eyes constantly swept the land on both sides and ahead as he drove. He estimated he had gone perhaps another ten miles and the moon was starting its downward path toward the horizon when he spotted the horseman at the edge of a line of canyon oak some fifty yards ahead. The rider began to move down the hill and Fargo's eyes flicked to the opposite slope, where he caught the movement that became two more riders moving toward him. No stetsons or ten-gallon hats on them, Fargo noted. All wore close-fitting fur hats, and as they reached the road and started toward him, he snapped the reins hard and the two horses surged forward.

They would stay racing in a straight line, well trained as they were, and he drew the Colt as he swung down onto the end of the long wagon shaft that ran between the two horses. Clinging with one hand to the shaft, the big rumps of the horses and the darkness all but hiding his figure, he saw the first two riders start to rein up as they saw no one holding the reins. His first shot caught the man on the left flush in the chest and he flew backwards from his horse. The second man fired three shots, all too hasty as he searched to find his quarry. Fargo fired two back as he clung to the bouncing shaft. The first struck the man high in the shoulder, but the second tore into his midsection and he bent in two, clung to his horse for a moment longer, and then fell to the ground.

Fargo saw the third rider turn and streak away. When the man disappeared, the horses began to slow their pace. Fargo pushed upwards, swung his body in a backward arc, and climbed up onto the driver's seat. He took the reins and brought the horses to a halt, leaped to the ground, and went to the nearest of the two men. He stared up at Fargo out of lifeless eyes, but he was very different from the other five—younger, his face strong with high cheekbones, and he wore a shirt with a high, round collar that was definitely Russian. Fargo stepped to where the other man lay on his stomach and turned him over to see he wore another of the Russian shirts and the peasant trousers that went only to the knee. He stirred and with his last breath muttered a handful of words, unmistakably Russian, before his eyes closed for the last time.

Fargo strode to the coach and yanked the door open to see the bearded man in pain on the floor. He reached in, helped him up on the seat where he breathed long, harsh draughts, each one causing him to groan in pain. "These were no highwaymen," Fargo said. "These were your people, Russians. You want to tell me what the hell's going on?"

"Get me to the house, please. We can talk there," Nicholas Rhesnev said, and he wasn't faking his agony. Fargo closed the door of the coach and climbed onto the driver's seat. The moon had slid behind the hills as he sent the team forward, his eyes peering into the darkness, searching for the third attacker. The man hadn't just fled, Fargo was certain. He was out there someplace, perhaps waiting, perhaps following, but he was there. The first streaks of dawn stretched across the sky, and he kept the coach thundering along the road as the morning broke. Dark masses of shadow became oaks and piñon pines, great vistas of deep dark took form as rock formations, and he could see clearly now. But he saw no horseman waiting, no sign of the man that had fled. He slowed, halted at a stream to let the horses drink, and then went on toward the expanse of thick forest that rose up ahead.

Skirting the heavy line of white fir, hackberry, and mountain ash, he followed a well-worn road until the buildings of the town came into sight. A weathered road sign proclaimed its name, CORNPIPE, and he had almost reached the first buildings of what was plainly a small, ramshackle town when he halted alongside a man with two mules loaded with prospector's tools. "Looking for Bear Trail," Fargo said, and the man, small and stooped, pointed to the left.

"That way. Take the first cut on your right," he said and eyed the coach. "Don't know that your rig's going to fit," he said.

"Much obliged," Fargo said and sent the team to the left until he spied the first cut in the road. The prospector had been almost right in his guess—the coach was barely able to take the narrow road. Tree branches hit against both sides of it as he moved down Bear Trail. The Ovaro fell back to trot along behind, and Fargo guessed he'd gone another mile when the trail widened slightly and he saw the house a hundred yards on, standing in a cleared patch of land alongside the trail. Two figures ran from the house as he drew to a halt in front of it with the coach, one a young man, tall, in a western shirt and dark trousers with a European cut to them, blond-haired with a clean-shaven face that would have been handsome except for a coldness in it and a cruel set to his mouth. The other figure was a young woman wearing a scoop-necked yellow peasant blouse and a full skirt. She too was blond, a dark blond, her hair braided and the two braids worn up around her head. Fargo took in a very attractive face, with broad, flat cheekbones, a straight nose, and a wide mouth with pale red lips. Brown eyes stared at him as the man strode to the coach.

"Where is Svetlov?" she asked, a faint accent in the words.

"Dead," Fargo grunted, and she frowned at once. She was about to ask him more, but she turned her attention to where the young man helped Nicholas Rhesnev from the coach. Rhesnev, his face contorted with pain, just managed to walk toward the house with the young man holding him up. The girl rushed to him, dismay clouding her face. Rhesnev spoke to her in Russian, and she raced into the house as the young man all but carried Rhesnev inside. Fargo stayed outside and leaned against the coach. Some ten minutes later she came from the house, hurrying toward him, and he watched the swing of full breasts under the blouse.

"Viktor is putting salve and bandages on his ribs," she said. "Nicholas told us what happened." She reached into a pocket in the skirt and brought out a roll of bills. "Here, fifty dollars. We are grateful for what you did." Her accent was less pronounced than Rhesnev's, but she displayed some of his imposing bearing in her slightly regal manner.

"Keep it. I didn't do it for the money," Fargo said, and

her eyebrows lifted. She studied his strong, chiseled handsomeness with a tiny furrow touching her smooth forehead.

"What you call a good deed?" she asked.

"What we call curiosity," Fargo said. "I'd like to know what this is all about."

The young woman's pale red lips pursed for a moment. "That is not for me to tell. Nicholas can tell you if he wishes to," she said.

"He owes me," Fargo said.

She thought for a moment. "Yes, perhaps he does, but that will be for him to decide," she said.

"Who are you?" Fargo questioned.

"Galina," she said, and a sudden smile made him realize that she was more than attractive and that behind the air of regality there was warmth.

"Galina," he echoed. "I've never known a Galina."

Her brown eyes suddenly danced. "I'll wager you've known every other woman's name," she said.

"Enough," he conceded.

"I've been wondering where the handsome cowboys were. Now I've found one," Galina said almost mischievously.

"I've heard that Russian girls can be very beautiful. Now I know that's true," Fargo returned, and she laughed, a low, husky sound. His eyes stayed admiringly on her, his attention thoroughly on her; but like the mountain lion, a part of him was always aware of things around him, an inner sense always tuned to his wild-creature hearing. The sound struck his ears and took a half-dozen seconds to translate itself: the stealthy rustle of leaves. "*Down!*" he yelled, even as he tackled Galina around the waist and carried her to the ground beneath him as the two shots cracked through the air and he felt the bullets whiz past. He rolled from her, yanking his Colt from its holster, but he heard the sound of branches being brushed back. The attacker was running, on foot. "Get in the house," he flung at Galina as he leaped to his feet and raced to the Ovaro.

Vaulting into the saddle, he sent the horse charging into the line of canyon oaks. The fleeing figure was still on foot, Fargo's ears told him, but he suddenly glimpsed a form through the trees as it leaped onto a horse. He swerved the pinto after the figure and saw the wool hat on the man, the third of the attackers who had fled . . . but not far. Fargo grunted with a kind of grim satisfaction at having been right. Being right had almost cost Galina her life, he realized as he took the Ovaro to the right of the fleeing horseman. The man's mount was having difficulty making time through the dense forest, Fargo saw, while the Ovaro's powerful hindquarters let it dodge and skirt trees with speed and agility. He was abreast of the man, who turned, raised a pistol, and fired, the heavy bullet gouging a big piece of wood from an oak that the Ovaro skirted.

The man fired again, but as he spurred his horse forward his next shot went wild. Fargo wheeled the Ovaro and headed straight for him, seeing the surprise on the man's face as he tried to fire another shot at the target that was now narrower. The surprise on his face changed to agonized pain as Fargo's shot caught him just below his ribcage. He pitched sideways from the horse, hit the ground, and was still before Fargo reached him. Fargo dropped to the ground and stared down at the man. He was definitely one of the last three, the round-collared shirt and a wide, sashlike belt completing the Russian attire marked by his tight wool hat. If he needed more proof, it was in the revolver lying on the ground, a center-fire, single-shot piece of definitely Russian make engraved with scenes of battle.

He picked it up, pushed it into his belt, and swung onto the Ovaro. When he reached the house, Galina came running from the door and her arms were around him the moment he dismounted. "*Spasibo, spasibo,*" she said.

"The one that got away," Fargo said. "But not this time."

She stepped back, her brown eyes searching his face. "You are indeed very special, Skye Fargo," she said.

"Rhesnev told you my name," he smiled, and she nodded. He handed her the pistol the man had held. "A gun from your country," he said.

"Yes," she nodded and pointed to writing at the end of the ornately carved butt. "It is a *Tula,* made by Goltiakov. He works for the Imperial court. The engraving shows the defense of Sebastopol against the British and French."

"It's time for answers, honey," Fargo said grimly.

"Yes. Nicholas is bandaged and ready to talk to you," Galina said, and she took his arm as she walked to the house with him. She had a light but firm touch, and he found himself wondering not so much about the strange set of events that had taken place, but what he might learn about Russian girls.

2

The bandages that wrapped Nicholas Rhesnev's torso might well have been a diplomat's sashes. They did not at all detract from his imposing bearing as he sat in a high-backed chair, his dark blue eyes clear and commanding. Nicholas Rhesnev was a tough old bird, Fargo decided. The very erect young man stood stiffly at Rhesnev's elbow, and Galina slouched on the arm of a deep leather chair. "Now you have saved Galina's life as well as mine, Fargo. I am doubly grateful to you," Rhesnev said and gestured to the young man at his side. "This is Viktor Nekharov. Viktor is my bodyguard." Fargo received a formal nod from Viktor Nekharov. "Galina tells me there are things you want to know," Rhesnev went on.

"Like the truth, for starters," Fargo said. "The first attack was no ordinary stage holdup and you know it. They were hired guns and they were definitely looking for something. The second three were your own people. They were backup, in place and waiting in case you got past the first attack. Now, what's this all about? You're not here sightseeing and visiting friends."

Nicholas Rhesnev winced with pain as he drew a deep breath. "You are right, my friend Fargo. I have not come here for pleasure," he said. "I came for a special reason, by boat from Vladivostok. I, Nicholas Rhesnev, am the first deputy aide to Alexander the Second, czar of all the Russias. Viktor is my bodyguard and Galina my assistant. We have come here to recover a priceless object stolen from the czar."

"All the way to Oregon to get back something stolen? It sure must be damn valuable," Fargo commented.

"It is not only priceless but very special," the man said.

"What the hell is it?" Fargo frowned.

"An Easter egg," Rhesnev said, and Fargo felt his brows go up as a furrow of incredulity dug into his forehead. "But it is not like any egg you have ever seen," the Russian said.

"It is a jeweled Easter egg designed by Gustave Fabergé," Galina's voice cut in. "Do you know who Gustave Fabergé is?"

"No."

Her little smile was condescending. "I didn't expect you would," she said.

"You know who Kit Carson is?" he asked.

"No," she said.

He returned the condescension with his own smile. "Didn't expect you would," he said.

Galina's eyes narrowed ever so slightly at him, but a quiet amusement flashed in their brown depths. "Touché," she said. "But so you may understand our purposes here, let me explain further. Gustave Fabergé is a master jeweler with a studio and shop on Bolshaya Morskaya Street in St. Petersburg, but his creations are known throughout Europe. He is the official jeweler of the Imperial family. They say his son Carl will be an even more outstanding artist and craftsman in time, but right now it is this jeweled Easter egg by the father, Gustave Fabergé, that the czar must have returned to him."

Nicholas Rhesnev spoke up. "It is made of green-gold

and red-gold enamel, rubies, diamonds, sapphires, and a base of matching pearls. Besides the priceless value of it, it is a first of its kind, a masterpiece of the jeweler's art. It can be held with one hand and is easy to conceal and transport."

"What do you know about the men who stole this?" Fargo questioned.

"A little. We have some information. They are thieves and killers, and our sources tell us they have come here to find a buyer," Rhesnev said.

Fargo turned the strange story over in his mind, a story almost too bizarre to believe, but he had seen the reality of it with his own eyes. But one question pushed itself at him. "Why didn't they try to sell it in Europe?" he asked. "Paris, Berlin, Rome. Why bring it all the way over here?"

"Czar Alexander has many friends and connections all over Europe. They would almost certainly be caught trying to sell it on the Continent. They decided that over here, in this land of millionaire Americans anxious to buy culture, they could find their buyer."

Fargo's thoughts leapfrogged. It had been a reasonable enough answer, one he couldn't fault, yet in the back of his mind something nagged at him—a feeling that the answer was not the whole truth. It was a vague, inner sense, and unable to define it, he decided to accept the explanation. "You have any leads on the men you're after?" he asked.

"A few. We know some of those involved, and our information tells us of certain moves they've made. We have to follow through on whatever we have, but now I'm too injured to carry on. We have discussed making an offer to you, Fargo," Rhesnev said. "You have said you are called the Trailsman and we have seen why. We will pay you handsomely to find these thieves and the jeweled egg for us, a thousand dollars in advance."

Fargo heard the low whistle escape his lips. "That's handsome, all right," he agreed.

"You will need someone to help you recognize them. I must keep Viktor here with me in case they make another attempt on my life. Galina will go with you. She is very capable, I assure you," the man said.

Fargo hesitated only a moment. The money was beyond turning down, and Galina was an intriguing addition, with her slightly imperious control and flashes of warmth. Besides, he was curious about a jeweled egg that could bring so many from so far away. "You've made a deal," he said. "Yes," he added as Rhesnev frowned. The man nodded in satisfaction, and at a word in Russian, Viktor handed Fargo a roll of bills. Not counting the money, Fargo slipped the bills into his pocket.

"It has been a long night for you. I'm sure you want to rest before starting out," Rhesnev said. "There is a bed in one of the two back rooms."

"I'll take an hour now and get a proper night's sleep tonight," Fargo said.

"As you wish," the man replied.

"I shall be outside and ready in an hour," Galina said to Fargo, who nodded and followed Viktor to a small room with a bed against one wall.

"A word of advice, my friend," the young Russian said as Fargo pulled off his boots. "Nicholas has sent Galina with you because he has no choice, but he expects you to watch out for her."

"I agreed to find this priceless egg, not to play nursemaid," Fargo said.

"It is not so much playing nursemaid as it is keeping

control of her. Galina can be very headstrong," Viktor said. "She likes to show her authority. I do not envy you."

"Does she have any authority?" Fargo smiled.

"She will be acting for Nicholas and she is his assistant. That is authority," Viktor said.

"Authority is important in your country, isn't it?" Fargo remarked.

"Yes. Is it not so here?" Viktor frowned.

"Only to make things run right. We don't worship authority. Nobody's born with it over here," Fargo said, and Viktor looked thoughtful as he closed the door and left. Fargo shed clothes, closed his eyes, and slept instantly. His inner clock woke him in an hour and he found a basin of water, washed and dressed, and went outside to see Galina beside a good, sturdy dun-colored quarter horse with a very large pack strapped across its rump. She wore tight-fitting riding britches of a cut he'd never seen before and a maroon blouse with white buttons down the center. The top buttons were opened to show the swell of full breasts, and he noticed she had a riding crop in one hand. "You're not going out for a pleasure ride," he muttered. "You're packin' a lot of stuff."

"Clothes. I came prepared for whatever might occur. I'm taking them because I don't know that I'll be back this way," she said.

"Rhesnev or Viktor could bring them," Fargo said.

"They have their own things," Galina ssaid. "The pack is not heavy. That's a solid horse. I'm told they are called quarter horses."

"Rhesnev brought his own coach and team. How come you didn't bring a horse for yourself?" Fargo asked as he swung onto the Ovaro.

"One of my fine Akhal Teké or my Karbardine stallions? Never. I had no idea what to expect of the terrain here," she said. "I decided it would be best to buy one of your homebreds."

He watched as she climbed onto the horse, her breasts swaying beautifully together. She moved well, he noted, a sure, light touch to her. "Actually, I was surprised to see that much of your land reminds me of Russia. It is both beautiful and rugged," she said, falling in beside him as he moved the Ovaro forward.

"Where are we going?" Fargo asked.

"A place called Eugene," Galina said. "You can find it, I assume."

"The least of our problems. We'll stay on the edge of the Willamette forest till we get near it," he said and turned the Ovaro northward. "You think they have your egg there?"

"Oh, no. They will have it hidden away somewhere. But our information tells us that three of the thieves are there, using it as a base. The three are led by a man named Krasnow. He is a big man with a red beard and he has been in trouble with the Moscow police before."

"You have any idea where to find him in Eugene?"

"No," Galina said curtly.

"Eugene is no cow town," Fargo said and drew a frown from her. "A small place where there are more cows than people," Fargo explained. "Eugene's become a fair-sized city with at least one fancy hotel. You ever hear the saying about looking for a needle in a haystack?"

"Yes, we use the expression in Russia. But that is why we hired you. You are the one who finds trails. You will be able to talk to your people in ways we could not. You will be accepted where we would not."

"That might be a way, but I'll think more on it," Fargo said. "You know what this man Krasnow looks like. Does he know you?"

"Probably," Galina said as Fargo turned along a road that bordered a very dense forest of blue spruce, silver fir, Engelmann spruce, and Rocky Mountain maple. He tossed her a quick glance.

"What does that mean?" he questioned.

"I am well known in Imperial society circles. My picture has been in newspapers," Galina said, and Fargo grunted to himself. It was more than probable that the men knew her—by sight, at least.

"You speak English very well. You all do. Where'd you learn it?" he asked.

"All members of the Imperial court and their families are taught French, German, and English," Galina said with a touch of superiority—perhaps not undeserved, Fargo conceded silently. He spied a stream bubbling its way a half-dozen yards into the forest and turned the Ovaro toward it.

"Let's water the horses and fill canteens," he said as he halted at the brook and swung from the saddle. Galina dismounted with a graceful, lithe motion, took her canteen, and dropped to her knees beside the water. The riding britches pulled tighter to outline shapely calves and long thighs, and he looked away as she pushed to her feet. But not quickly enough, he realized, seeing the cool amusement in her eyes. "Rhesnev said you were very capable. What'd he mean exactly?" Fargo asked.

"He meant I am a fine pistol shot and a number one horsewoman. I have also been taught to be an excellent fencer," she said. "Why do you ask?"

"I want to know if I have to protect your ass or if you really can take care of yourself," he tossed at her.

"Crude but to the point," Galina sniffed. "I assure you I can protect my ass."

"I'll concede you can ride well, but there'll be damn

little chance you'll get to use a sword, so let's see if you can really shoot a pistol," Fargo said and drew his Colt and handed it to her.

"I prefer a gun I'm used to," she said, reached into her saddlebag, and pulled out a long-barreled pistol with engraved scrollwork on the grip. "This is another model *Tula,* the one used by the cossacks," she said.

Fargo's eyes swept the forest and came to rest on a long line of rose crowns, each pink stalk rising upwards individually, silhouetted against the sky. "I count twelve," he said. "Let's see how many of the first six you can hit and how fast."

She shot him a half-amused glance. "Very small targets at a good distance," she commented.

"Too small for you?" he slid at her.

"I didn't say that. I've beaten the best of the czar's personal guards in target shooting," Galina said as she raised the pistol and squeezed the trigger. Fargo watched her fire with steady, even pacing, and when she finished, four of the first six rose crowns were gone.

"Fair," Fargo said and drew an instant frown.

"Fair? It was excellent," Galina said.

"Pretty good marksmanship, but too slow," he said.

Her eyes flashed dark fire. "I'd like to see you do better," Galina challenged.

"Little side bet?" he said, and she frowned in perplexity. "Wager," he explained.

"Yes," she said, her chin lifting.

"What?" he asked.

"A gentleman's wager, purely for the sport of it," she said. His nod held an edge of disdain, but Galina kept cool insistence in her eyes.

Fargo turned to peer at the distant line of rose crowns, paused a moment, then drew the Colt and fired, all in one smooth, lightning-fast motion, six shots fired with such speed the sound blended into one. When the last reverberation died away, six of the rose crown stalks were gone, and he heard Galina's tiny gasp. He tossed a glance at her as he reloaded. She was still staring at the target, but turned to bring her eyes to his, wide and filled with awe.

"Stupendous. Really astounding," she said, and he saw a new appreciation in her eyes.

"I should've insisted on a bet," Fargo said.

"In my circle it is the custom that a lady's smile of approval is considered reward enough," Galina said with a touch of reproof.

"This isn't your circle. We've different customs here," he said, holstering the Colt.

"Such as?"

He moved quickly, one arm half-circling her waist, and he pulled her to him and his lips were on hers, feeling their firm warmth and the touch of her breasts against his chest. She didn't respond but she didn't pull away, and he stepped back after a moment. "Such as that," he said. "Now you've got to agree that's a much better custom."

Her cool composure remained. "I'll have to think about that," she said.

"Hell you do," he laughed and saw the faint flush touch her high cheekbones. He pulled himself onto the Ovaro and set out. She came alongside him in moments.

"The men I know do not speak to me that way," Galina said stiffly.

"How do they speak to you?" Fargo asked.

"With a great deal more deference," she sniffed.

"Different worlds, different ways," he said. "You know you've never told me your whole name."

"Galina Rhesnev," she said, and Fargo felt his brows go up as the surprise grabbed him.

"Nicholas is your father?" he frowned, and she nodded. "You said you were his assistant."

"I am. I work for him at the czar's palace. That is why I'm here, not just because I am his daughter."

"Why didn't you tell me?" Fargo questioned.

"It was not important," she said loftily. Fargo nodded at the answer but the inner question swept through him again. Was there more to all this than he'd been told? What other "not important" things were being held back? But he kept the questions to himself and cast an eye at a sky rapidly growing gray.

"Ride," he said and put the Ovaro into a trot, pushing aside the moment of discomfort that had swept through him. Galina caught up to him. She rode the horse well, he noted, her body fluid and at ease with her mount, her breasts hardly swaying.

It began to be a contest as to which would descend first, the rain or the dusk, and the rain won. It became a steady downpour that quickly grew heavier. After a pause to don rain gear, he continued northward, still edging the dense forest. The dusk had begun to close down, helped by the heavy rain, and he could feel the ground already softening under the Ovaro's hooves. He rode on another half hour, then he halted and swept the terrain with his eyes in the last light.

The dense forest was at his right, and to his left the land rose in a steep slope. He saw a thick-domed overhang some fifty yards up the slope. "There, a place to keep dry," Galina said, spotting the overhang as he did.

Fargo's eyes stayed narrowed as he peered through the rain. "We'll take the forest. That blue spruce and Rocky

Mountain maple is so dense it'll keep out a lot of the rain."

"Not like that overhang will," Galina said.

Fargo peered hard for a moment longer. "We'll take the woods," he said.

"I don't like sleeping in rain. We'll take the overhang," Galina said crisply.

"The woods," he said with dismissive flatness.

"Fargo, you've been hired to find a trail, not to give orders," Galina said imperiously.

"You don't usually get orders, I take it," he said.

"That's right," she sniffed.

"Too bad. I'm taking the woods," he said.

"That's just childish stubbornness. I won't indulge it," she snapped and sent her horse forward. He watched her go up the slope and fade from sight, just before she reached the overhang, in the curtain of driving rain. He swore softly. He'd never been exposed to Russian bitchiness. There wasn't any difference that he could see, except that she added an imperiousness to it. He turned the Ovaro into the forest and was instantly swallowed up by blackness. The rain came down but without the driving fury, and he halted, swung to the ground, and felt his way to the saddlebag, where he pulled out a large square of tarpaulin. Feeling his way amid the trees, he took a half hour to secure the tarpaulin to the low branches by the rawhide tie strings at each corner. Finally he had a canvas roof that kept out all the rain.

Again, he swore softly to himself as he took his lariat from the saddle and made his way to the edge of the trees. Again, working by feel more than sight in the rain-driven blackness, he wrapped one end of the lariat around a tough spruce trunk and walked a dozen yards to wrap the other end around another trunk. He turned, then, and using his honed senses and mental imagery, he trudged east to the slope and knew he was on the right track when he felt the soft ground rise upwards steeply under his feet. Pausing every few feet to wipe the rain from his eyes, he climbed the increasing steepness of the slope. Halting, he strained his eyes as he searched the blackness in the pelting rain and finally saw it, blackness against blackness, a black bulk that rose up just ahead of him.

He climbed toward it, fell as the earth slid out from under his feet, dug his hands down and halted his slide. Moving with slow steps, digging his feet down with each one, he began to climb again. He heard the sucking sound of mud sliding past him on both sides, some of it grasping at his ankles as he shook it away. He heard the two sounds almost as one: the low rumble of earth falling, collapsing under the weight of the rain, and then the scream of pure fright. It came from directly in front of him, and then he glimpsed the form moving past him to his right, the horse half-running and half-sliding down the slope.

Her scream came again as he felt the mound of earth go past him. "I'm here," he shouted. "Let yourself go. Slide." She answered, words in Russian, but he heard her cry of despair and he was squinting, straining his eyes as he peered upwards, searching through the sheet of rain. He glimpsed her, finding her more by her cries at first, then discerning the sliding shape a few feet to his right. He half-slid, half-dived, caught hold of her and felt her arms wrap around him. "Don't fight. Go with it," he said and let himself be carried downwards with her. When he felt the slope leveling off and the mud growing higher, he dug in, pushed to his feet, and pulled her with him. Crawling, slipping, using hands and feet, he pulled her with him across the accumulated wall of mud at the bottom of the slope until, on level ground, he was able to walk with one arm around her waist. With a silent prayer he hadn't lost his bearings, he struck out in a straight line and finally the dark mass of the forest rose up. Reaching out, he felt the air with one hand and uttered a cry of relief as his fingers closed around the lariat that stretched taut along the trees.

He untied the end and followed the rope to the other end, where he untied that knot, turned sharply left, and gratefully trudged into the woods, where the rain was only a soft, steady downfall. He found the canvas shelter and sank to the ground with Galina still clutching him. He lay there under the tarpaulin roof and let breath slowly return. He finally sat up, and as he did, the sound of raindrops on the canvas suddenly ceased.

"It's over. It's passed on," he said. "Storms are that way here at this season. They hit suddenly and leave just as suddenly. The moon will be out in another ten minutes."

"It all came down over me," she said, and he listened, unable to see her. They were, he reflected, as two disembodied voices in the blackness. "I'd be buried under the earth and mud except for you. I owe you my life and I want to be grateful, but I'm angry. You knew this would happen," she said.

"Not for sure. If it had stopped raining it wouldn't have happened," he said.

"But you felt it would happen," she accused.

"The overhang was all earth, no rock in it," he said, the answer an admission.

"And you let me go."

"I told you not to go. You said not to give you orders, remember, honey?"

"That was rotten."

"Look, princess, I didn't have to come after you. You cash it in? Job's over. I have my money," he said. She was silent and he wished he could see her face. Finally she answered, her voice somehow smaller.

"I'm sorry. I did not think of it that way. I've been very wrong. Please forgive me," she said.

"Consider it done," he grunted.

"You can give me orders whenever you like," she said. A sudden, very pale light filtered through the trees, enough for him to see her. The moon had come out, almost exactly ten minutes later, and Galina took shape beside him, her hair and face streaked with mud.

"You need some cleaning up," he said.

"So do you," she replied.

"A douse of rain can do it," he said, pushing to his feet.

"The rain has stopped," Galina said.

"Watch," he said and pulled off his rain gear, then his shirt and trousers, keeping on only underpants. He stepped from beneath the canvas, stood under the trees, and shook the lower branches. A cascade of rainwater came down instantly, and he washed himself free of mud in its cool shower. When he stepped back under the canvas, Galina was standing, her eyes moving up and down the muscled contours of his torso. "There's plenty more left. Pick another tree," he told her.

"I want to but I'm not about to put on a display," she said. "You could promise not to watch," she said.

"And if I don't promise?"

"I'll stay covered with mud until I can find a place to bathe tomorrow," she said firmly, and then, the tone of her voice changing again, "Please promise." Her tone was suddenly soft. She used her voice well, he noted. She could go from stiff to soft, prim properness to warm pleading in an instant.

"You're asking a lot," he said. "No promises, but I'll try." She rose to her feet and hurried from under the canvas as he went to his saddlebag and pulled out a towel. He heard her undressing, shaking the tree, and the water cascading down. The Ovaro moved, and as he reached out to steady the horse, he couldn't help but glimpse her rubbing the mud from herself. He caught a flash of a full, sturdy figure, a very round rear, and deep breasts, and he forced himself to pull his eyes away. He'd half-promised and he'd play at being a gentleman. Or a damn fool, he muttered to himself.

She was holding her clothes in front of herself when she stepped back under the tarpaulin roof, and he tossed her the big towel. "Thank you," she said as she wrapped herself in the towel. "Everything's with my horse and he's gone."

"Not far. He'll be back come morning. He's an old hand. He won't wander far," Fargo said as he settled himself half into his bedroll. "There's room for two," he said.

"You said it was asking a lot for you not to watch. This would be asking even more," she said, sudden laughter in her dark eyes. "I'll just stay wrapped in the towel."

"Your call," he said, settling down. He watched her lie down close beside him, her bare, round shoulders very lovely. He lay back, closed his eyes, then frowned as he felt her hand on his. He turned and she was on her side, looking at him.

"Perhaps I called wrong, Fargo," she said. "You are very special. I would not want to take back just ordinary memories of you."

"What do you want to take back?" he asked.

"The memories that come from the senses, from touching, feeling, holding, the memories that become a part of you for all time," she said.

He sat up, reached out, rested one finger on the top of the towel. She made no move to push his hand away, and he pulled on the towel. It came off and fell to her waist as Galina sat up. His eyes held on the beautifully full, round breasts, each tipped with a pale red, almost flat little nipple against a circle of pink. A round, strong rib cage rose just below her deep breasts, and as he watched, Galina reached up, loosened the twin braids, and her hair fell down around her shoulders in a cascade of yellow-gold. She moved, the rest of the towel fell away, and he saw fully rounded hips, smoothly contoured thighs, and a nap that was almost as blond as the loose hair encircling her high-cheekboned face.

She reached her arms out, came to him, and her smooth fullness was against him, deep breasts pillowy against his chest, her lips on his, her mouth open, letting him taste of her tongue. "*Da, da,*" she murmured. "Who knows what tomorrow may bring? I cannot turn away tonight, now, you." He brought his face down and nuzzled between the full, deep breasts, letting his lips find one pale pink tip, letting his tongue gently circle it. "Oh, oh, *da, da,*" Galina murmured and pushed upwards, offering him more of the round, soft mound. He took it, drew it deeper into his mouth, and felt the almost flat nipple grow firmer, taller, and he caressed it with his tongue. "*Khorosho . . . khorosho* . . . good, good," she moaned, and her fingers dug into his shoulders. She half-turned, bringing her body against his, the blond nap pressing into his groin. "Ah, ah, aaaaah . . . ," she said and cried out as his hand slid downwards, across the small mound of her belly, down into the blond triangle. "Oh, yes, yes . . . *da, da . . . khorosho,*" Galina gasped.

She turned onto her back, offering the fullness of her beauty to him, and her lips were open, tiny gasping sounds coming from them, her eyes half-closed as his hand pressed through the soft-firm nap, slid down further, traced a warm path along the inner curve of her thighs, and found the moistness of her skin. She pressed her thighs together, caught his hand in between, and held him there until she let her legs fall open, her little whimpered sounds timeless entreaties. His hand moved upwards, slowly, reached the sweet portal and touched the moist threshhold and Galina's hips twisted as she moaned. He caressed the liquescent lips and her moan became a scream of ecstasy. He felt her hand come over his, pressing him deeper, and she was writhing as she moaned and gasped for air. Her hand moved, closing around his pulsating warmth, and her scream of delight pierced the night air.

"*Dahite mne . . . dahite mne . . . poojalasta.* Give me . . . please, please," she half-screamed, and her hips rose, the body crying out, the language of the flesh. Her hand around him pulled at him, brought him to her warm wetness, the welcoming wine of ecstasy, and Galina gave a low, undulating moan as he slid into her. Softly fleshy thighs rose, came against his hips, held tight there, embrace of the flesh, and he moved slowly in her, increasing his sliding thrusts. Galina was making moaning sounds, each ending with a gasp of breath. "Ah, ah, *yestcho . . . yestcho* . . . more, more," she called out, and her blond hair flew from side to side as she twisted her head and shoulders with the pleasures of her ecstasy. Her full hips rose, thrust upwards with his movements, and she was babbling words in Russian that needed no translating. Her full-fleshed body was almost rolling with him, every part of her totally immersed in the passion of flesh to flesh, wetness to wetness, warmth to warmth.

As her excitement increased she clung tighter to him,

her gasping moans rising. Suddenly he felt the tremors inside her, softness throbbing around him, sweet contractions, and Galina's deep breasts were shaking furiously as her torso twisted from side to side, blond hair swishing back and forth. "*Daaaaa . . . oh, daaaaa, oh, oooooh,* it is now . . . now . . . noooow," she said and screamed and screamed, a glorious, wild sound full of ecstasy and overwhelming passion. After the last of it died away, she continued to stay wrapped around him. He held her full-bodied form, her breasts flattened against him, and she pulled him down to the bedroll with her, her lips parted, brown eyes staring up at him as though she were trying to see through him. "I never expected this would happen over here," she murmured, still holding tight to him.

"You sorry?" Fargo asked.

"No, the unexpected is often the best," Galina said as she relaxed her hold on him and he sank down beside her. "And it would never have happened in my homeland, not like this."

"Why not?"

"Too many things would have stood in the way. But this is a sign," she said, pulling his hand to press against one soft, deep breast.

"A sign?" he echoed with a frown.

"It means it is good that we met. It means you are good for me, for what I must do. You will recover the egg," she said. "Now we must sleep so we can ride with the sun."

"You sure?" he asked, rubbing one pale pink tip. "There might not be another time."

She thought for a moment. "I will find a time," she said. "Perhaps before we've finished, perhaps after, but I will find a time."

He settled down beside her soft warmness. Galina was

a young woman of dedication. She kept her eye firmly on the ball . . . in this case the egg. He admired that. But he'd find another time and place if she didn't. That was certain . . . probably the only thing that was.

3

She had her hair up in the two braids circling her face and didn't look nearly as wanton, the simmering volcano he had discovered replaced by cool control again. But her loveliness remained, the high-cheekboned face radiantly beautiful in the morning sun as they rode. She had put on a fresh deep green blouse with a scoop neck and puffy sleeves that hinted at her homeland, and she hadn't mentioned the night before, he noted with an inward smile. He kept the Ovaro heading northward and swung to the west only when he glimpsed the blue ribbon of the Willamette River. Eugene came into sight soon after, but the day was more than half over by then. Eugene's streets were crowded with Owensboro farm wagons rubbing wheels with Peabody Victorias, with a sprinkling of surreys and light pony wagons thrown in. His eyes swept the figures riding and walking the streets as he rode slowly toward the center of town with Galina.

"It is as crowded as you said it would be," she observed. "But it should not be so difficult to find out about three foreigners."

"Take another look around you," Fargo said as they pressed through the crowded streets. She followed his eyes as they paused at a dozen Chinese, a goodly number of Mexicanos up from California, a group of French fur trappers in their distinctive beaver hats and colorful kerchiefs, some very well dressed Europeans in landaus—probably German, he guessed—and a half-dozen men in what were unmistakably Russian seaman's clothes.

"I had no idea," Galina murmured in astonishment.

"Eugene attracts a lot of visitors who come down the Willamette and by coach from the coast. It'll be a waste of time asking about your three men, even one with a red beard," Fargo said. "That's probably why they picked Eugene."

"Then what do we do? Just search for them?"

"That could take too long. I've been thinking while we rode. You can't find the fox, you bring the fox to you," Fargo said. Galina frowned at him. "We'll use bait," he said, and her frown deepened. "Decoy," he tried. "You know what a decoy is?"

"For hunting ducks," she said.

"Bulls-eye," Fargo said. "You'll be the decoy, the bait. This man Krasnow will know you, you said."

Galina nodded. "If he sees me he'll know why I am here."

"Perfect. You'll be the bait that will lead us to the egg," Fargo said.

"But Krasnow is not top man. We know that," Galina said.

"He can lead us to the top man."

"Yes, probably," she said. "This is sounding exciting."

"It'll be a lot more than exciting. It'll be dangerous."

"I'm not afraid of that. I expect danger," she said with cool assuredness. He nodded and drew to a halt before the largest building in Eugene as dusk neared. Its columned facade was lighted with ornate lamps, and two white-frame stories featured tall arched windows alongside a wide doorway. A sign hung over the doorway,

HOTEL EUGENE, and Fargo counted four sedan brougham closed hansom cabs lined up outside, their drivers waiting for fares. A long hitching bar ran along one side of the hotel.

"You got a fancy dress inside that travel bag?" Fargo asked.

"Yes," Galina said.

"Take your things," he said as he drew up to the hitching post, dismounted, and tethered both horses. "We'll get adjoining rooms," he said.

"I will pay. I've money to be used for this," Galina said.

"I won't argue," Fargo said and followed her into the carpeted lobby of the hotel and to the front desk, where a clerk in a formal jacket greeted them. "Two rooms, adjoining," Fargo said, and Galina took out her purse to pay. She signed in and Fargo signed beneath her. A bellboy appeared and led them through the lobby, where a huge chandelier added a note of opulence. Fargo noted the formal dining room, with its gleaming white linen tablecloths and fine china. He also took in the three entrances to the room and the tall Indian rubber plants that decorated the corners. Their rooms were at the end of a wide corridor on the first floor, and Fargo helped Galina carry her bags into hers.

"Here's the plan," he said when they were alone. "You dress up and go down to dinner. Make heads turn. It might draw Krasnow tonight, or it might take a couple of nights. But I think it'll draw him. When you've finished dinner, come back here to your room. If Krasnow sees you, it'll be damn sure he'll come after you."

"He might decide to take me to Pavlev," Galina said.

"Pavlev?"

"We believe he is the brains behind it all, what you call the top man. Igor Pavlev."

"Then he's the one we want. Let him take you," Fargo said. "You won't be seeing me, but I'll be watching every damn minute. I'll be watching you at dinner, and when you come back, I'll be next door listening. If they take you I'll be there, following. When the time's right, I'll move in, and we'll have this Pavlev and your egg."

"Yes, that is the important thing. Getting the egg back is all that matters," Galina said with a sudden firmness.

"Are you afraid to be a decoy?" he asked.

"No, not with you watching over me," she said, and her lips were suddenly on his, sweet softness, and then she pulled away.

"Go to dinner at eight," he told her as he opened the door that led to the adjoining room. "Lock it and then talk in a normal voice," he said and stepped into the other room and closed the door. He halted, leaned his ear to the door, and heard Galina's voice more than clearly enough. Satisfied, he allowed himself a confident smile and stretched out on the bed in the dark as night fell. He relaxed, napped some, and finally rose and sat up. He lit a kerosene lamp and freshened his face with the water in a deep porcelain bowl on the dresser. When he left the room, a large clock in the corridor told him it was fifteen minutes to eight, and he strolled toward the dining room. It was quite filled with well-dressed people dining leisurely. He took in the three entranceways to the dining room.

A corridor connected all three, he noted. Two of the open doorways simply led from the room and the third connected to the kitchen, where waiters scurried back and forth with trays. It was the third one, where a particularly large and thick plant grew, that afforded the best view of the room and the other two entrances, so he moved through the corridor to take up a position behind the plant. He drew quick, curious glances from the waiters that passed, but no one said anything to him and he relaxed against the side of the doorway and let his eyes sweep the dining room.

Well hidden behind the tall plant, he surveyed each table and found no one with a red beard. Most of the tables were occupied by couples or parties of five or six diners, all well dressed, many in evening clothes. His glance had paused at a table of six when he saw their heads turn to the main doorway. He followed their gaze and felt his own breath draw in sharply. The young woman framed in the door was a living picture of regal beauty, twin braids enclosing a face subtly painted and powdered to enhance its every feature, graceful long neck emphasized by the bare-shouldered gown of deep, royal blue, the neckline so low only the ruffles obscured the curve of her breasts. He stared, as did everyone else in the room, as she swept forward, the floor-length gown making it seem as if she walked on air. The restaurant manager rushed forward to pull a chair out for Galina as she sat down at a small table against the far wall.

He had seen the regal beauty of her from their very first meeting, but now he could really see her at the Imperial court of the czar. Now she exuded an added dimension that was made up of equal parts of imperiousness, disdain, and beauty that made her seem above anything so crass as an orgasm. Only he knew better. Yet she was a very different Galina now, and he decided he liked the other one better; her beauty here was edged with ice. After her entrance, the dining room settled back to normalcy and Fargo watched Galina order a drink and dinner. The drink turned out to be red wine. From his hiding place, he continued to survey the room and the entrances. Galina had just finished dinner when Fargo saw the man watching her from behind another tall plant, much as he'd been doing.

The man wore a loose jacket over a full blouse with a round, high, tight-necked collar plainly of Russian design, and he sported a black mustache. After staring at Galina, he abruptly turned and hurried away. Fargo held his place and bided time and was rewarded when, as Galina paid her check, the man reappeared, this time with a second man. The second man, a burly figure, wore a deep red beard. Both men peered at Galina and then quickly left. "Bulls-eye," Fargo muttered and left his hiding place to see the bearded one hurry across the lobby, the other man following. They halted at the other side of the lobby, where they met with two more men—these two unmistakably American, wearing Levi's, checkered shirts, six-guns, and wide-brimmed Stetsons. More hired hands, Fargo murmured to himself. They conversed quickly, the bearded one's hands moving in agitated little gestures. Then one of the two Americans hurried from the hotel. The other joined the bearded man as he went to the front desk. He was examining the register ledger when Fargo turned and stepped behind a pillar as Galina swept from the dining room and headed down the corridor to her room.

He stayed, watched her go, and saw the bearded man's eyes following, also watching her go down the corridor. The man moved for a better view of Galina and saw her enter her room. He turned to the other three and all hurried from the hotel. Fargo took the moment to step from behind the pillar and head for the room adjoining Galina's in long-legged strides. He entered, pulled a chair close to the door that separated the two rooms, and sat down to wait. It had happened quicker than he'd dared to expect. They had seen the bait. Now they'd take it, he was certain. They might even bring this Pavlev with them, Fargo mused. Galina would have shed the fancy gown by now, and the thought of her full-breasted body brought a smile of remembrance to him.

He didn't dare risk trying to alert her. The others could appear at any moment. Her surprise would make them confident, and that was important. He had just leaned forward in the chair when he heard the knock at the door of Galina's room and heard her call out, "Yes?"

"Hotel manager, ma'am," the voice said, unmistakably American. One of their hired hands, Fargo thought.

"Just a moment," Galina said, and Fargo pressed his ear to the door, heard her open hers, and then heard her sharp cry of dismay, followed by a rush of footsteps and a sharp slap. Galina cried out again, and he heard her fall to the floor. She spoke in Russian and someone answered in Russian, an exchange of sharp, angry words, and then Galina's voice was protesting, gasping in pain, words that were curses in any language. Suddenly someone spoke in accented English.

"Now we get her out of here," he said. "Pavlev will want to question her himself."

"Everything's ready, Krasnow," the answer came from one of the Americans. "We've got the coach waiting. Driver's all paid. There's a side door from this place. We'll take her out that way."

Fargo rose at once, crossed to the door, and strode into the corridor, where he broke into a run on silent feet. He skirted the lobby as he ran from the hotel, his eyes scanning the hansom coaches lined up as he rounded the corner and crossed the narrow alleyway to melt into the deep shadows on the other side. He saw the coach waiting along the side of the hotel, a sedan cab, tightly closed, with the driver sitting in the open up front and entry through a rear door. Two small lamps were fastened to the front of the cab, and he noticed that one was broken. He had but a few minutes to wait until the side door of the hotel opened and the three figures emerged, one carrying a black sack over his shoulder. When another opened the rear door of the coach, he threw the sack inside and slammed the door shut.

"On your way," he called to the coach driver. "You got your pay and your orders." Fargo heard the driver snap his whip over the horse and the coach rolled off at once. He stayed in the shadows, his hand on the butt of the Colt, but he didn't draw the gun. Krasnow and his hired hands weren't the prize. It was the man, Pavlev, and bound and no doubt gagged inside the sack, Galina would lead him to Pavlev. Fargo watched the three men dissappear back into the hotel before he ran up the alleyway to where the Ovaro waited at the hitching post. Vaulting into the saddle, he wheeled the horse in a tight circle and rode after the coach. He came in sight of it quickly enough, though the coachman was driving hard as he headed away from Eugene under a three-quarter moon.

Fargo hung back and let the coach move beyond his sight as he followed the sound of the bouncing wheels and creaking chassis. Once clear of Eugene, the driver stayed on the road until he reached a hilly terrain that was part of the Willamette forest area. He turned and began to take the coach into the low hills that were thickly covered with heavy growths of Norway spruce, hackberry, and mountain ash, a tricky terrain where the moonlight showed deep ravines amid the hills. He was in sight of the coach, following as the driver went left along a barely wide enough trail, then turned north, and finally east along a level ridgeline.

Fargo continued to trail the coach and felt a frown starting to dig into his brow. When the coach driver turned from the ridgeline and seemed to double back along a wandering moose trail, the frown dug in deeper. The man was driving the coach all over the hills, driving in an aimless pattern, and Fargo spurred the Ovaro forward. Perhaps he had gotten himself lost. If so, he'd know where he had been told to go, Fargo considered. It was time to find out. He sent the Ovaro down a slope that brought him out in front of the coach as it rounded a curve in the trail. The Colt in his hand, he blocked the path. The driver reined to a halt at once, putting his hands into the air, as Fargo moved alongside the coach. "No gun, friend . . . no gun," he said, a round-faced man with a battered top hat that allowed patches of gray hair to stick out from under its brim.

"Get down," Fargo ordered, and the man swung from the driver's seat. "Lay down on the ground, facedown," Fargo snapped, and the man obeyed at once.

"Yes, sir," he muttered, fear in his voice.

"Stay there. Don't move," Fargo ordered as he swung from the pinto and strode to the rear door of the coach. He'd take Galina out of the suffocating sack before he questioned the driver. Pulling the door open, he saw the sack on the floor of the coach, the figure inside with knees drawn up under the black fabric. Holstering his gun, he reached into the coach and used both hands to untie the drawstring at the top of the sack. Pulling it down at both sides, he had time only to glimpse the face and the pistol pointing out at him when the gun went off. The searing pain shot across the side of his temple and the blinding flash shut out all vision. He fell backwards and then there was no more, the world becoming instant blackness.

4

It had happened in an instant, and the terrible cognizance of death had flashed before him in the last, fleeting second before he was engulfed in the void of nothingness. Time ended, all at once. Time and life itself? There was no way to ask. The dead cannot ask, cannot question, cannot call out for one more moment. They can only lie and wait for answers beyond giving on this earth. They are beyond the senses of life, beyond seeing, hearing, smelling, tasting, or touching. They are beyond feeling cold or hot, soft or rough. Yet Fargo felt a coldness, a wet coldness. It was a sudden thing, coming after seconds, minutes, hours?

But it was there. How much does the fabric of life imprint itself upon the subconscious? he was to wonder later, for it was not so much a sensation, a dim realization, but he saw it as a signpost that the trail hadn't ended once and for all. He was alive and he let the magnificence of that fact seep through him. Slowly, he felt something more, his eyelids fluttering, finally coming open. There was only grayness at first, and then light began to filter through the gray haze, slowly shredding the mist, and then the light became an irregular, fuzzy form. It slowly took shape and became a rock lying only a few feet from him. The rest of his body began to wake. He found he could move fingers, hands, arms as strength slowly returned to his muscles.

He lifted his head, groaned in pain, fell back onto his side, and stared upwards. A sharp slope of land rose up, and turning his head despite the pain, he saw another sharp slope. He was at the bottom of a ravine, and he turned again to see he lay in a small rivulet of water, much of it stained red. He lowered the side of his head into the water again and now felt the cooling, soothing comfort. More blood stained the water from one side of his head, and he lay there resting, realizing the dawn had come up. He finally sat up, used his kerchief to pat the side of his face dry, and felt the blood still caulked against his skin. Thoughts began to return to him, last moments reliving themselves. Hours had gone by, he realized, and he uttered a curse as he realized he'd been thoroughly and completely outwitted.

They had suspected someone might be watching Galina. They'd seen through the bait and had turned it around on him. He cursed again. He had completely underestimated them, and as he blamed himself, he realized with a grim and new awareness that he had been dealing with men from a land where intrigue and counterintrigue were a way of life. He was an amateur in the intrigue business, compared to them. Yet he should have realized that, he chastised himself angrily. It was a lesson he'd remember, he vowed. Slowly, wincing with the pain that still shot through the one side of his face, he pushed to his feet. The rest of what had happened was easy enough to reconstruct. The man in the sack had emerged and thought his shot had killed. With the aid of the driver—though perhaps not, Fargo pondered—he had been thrown into the ravine and left for dead.

Ignoring the pain still in his body, he began to climb

the steep side of the ravine, using tough bunches of brush to pull himself up, pausing to rest every few feet as his strength still hadn't fully returned. Finally he pulled himself over the top and lay there, taking in deep gasps of air until he pushed to his knees and felt the rest of his strength slowly surging through him. He whistled, once, twice, three times, suddenly heard the sound of hoofbeats, and the black-and-white form appeared through the trees in the new morning sun. He pulled himself onto the horse and slowly rode through the hills, finding a small pond where he halted, stripped, and immersed himself in the water. He washed the blood from his face and neck, washed more from his shirt, and used a towel from his saddlebag to dry himself. Finally, in clean, dry clothes, he was in the saddle again, heading down from the hills, at a fast trot now.

Of all that had happened, the one thing that stabbed hardest at him was the promise he'd made Galina. The words came back at him again: *I'll be there, watching, waiting, following. I'll be there.* Her answer dug into him. She wasn't afraid, she had said, *Not with you watching over me.* The words burned through him and he swore silently. He hadn't watched over her. His promise had been hollow. Instead, he'd fallen into their trap. The angry bitterness rode with him toward Eugene. The coach and driver had been among the hansoms waiting at the hotel. That was his one lead. The afternoon sun was still high when he reached the busy, crowded streets of Eugene. He halted at the hotel, dismounted, and strode to the front desk, where the clerk was not the same man as the night before. "Single, sir?" the clerk asked. He was a prim-faced, small man.

"Just some answers," Fargo said. "There was a line of hansom cabs waiting outside the hotel last night. I lost something in one of them, but I can't remember which one. You know the cabs and drivers?"

"Just the regulars," the clerk replied.

"I want a cab with a broken light," Fargo said.

"That'd be Mickey Ryan. We've been on him to get that light fixed for a month," the man smiled.

"Where'll I find him?" Fargo asked.

"End of Wagon Street. He's got a house and stable there."

"There was a young woman who registered last night, Galina Rhesnev. She still here?" Fargo asked blandly.

The clerk consulted his register book. "No, that's the woman the night clerk told me about. It seems she took sick and passed out. Some friends of hers took her to find a doctor," he said.

"Much obliged," Fargo said and hurried from the hotel and pulled himself onto the Ovaro. Asking directions of a passing freight-wagon driver, he found Wagon Street at the outskirts of the city. At the end of it, he saw the house and stable with the unhitched coach outside. He dismounted and went to the front door, pounding on it with his hand on the butt of his Colt. There was no answer and he pounded again. There was still no answer, and he closed one hand around the doorknob and turned it. The door came open and he stepped into a dim, cluttered room with worn furniture. "Ryan?" he called, and silence was the only answer. "Ryan, you in here?" he called again, and once more there was only silence. He stepped around the clutter toward a second room that turned out to be filled with boxes, crates, harnesses, extra carriage wheels, and other assorted gear.

He was about to leave when he glimpsed the foot sticking out from behind a long crate. Kicking a box out of the way, he rushed to the spot to see the coach driver lying facedown on the floor. "Shit," he swore as he turned the man over and saw his red-soaked chest. But somehow he was breathing, Fargo saw as he knelt down. He spied a horse blanket nearby and pushed it under the man's head. "Ryan, can you hear me?" he asked. "Ryan?" He gently slapped the man's face and saw the coachman's eyelids tremble, come open, and stare at him. Ryan's lips worked for a moment before sound came from them.

"Doc . . . get me to a doc," he managed to say.

Fargo glanced at the man's shattered chest, the result of at least three bullets, and wondered how the man was still alive. There was damn little chance he'd make it to a doctor, Fargo knew, his mouth a grim line. "Talk to me first. What happened after the bastard threw me into the ravine?" he asked.

Ryan coughed as he found words wrapped in pain. "I drove him back to the hotel," Ryan said.

"Then you took them someplace else, with the girl," Fargo said, and Ryan nodded with a groan. "Where?" Fargo demanded.

"Red house . . . on river."

"The Willamette?" Fargo pressed.

Ryan managed another nod. "Doc . . . I need a doc," he gasped, his voice a rattling sound.

"Hold onto me," Fargo said as he stepped behind the man and began to lift him to his feet. Ryan swayed and would have fallen had Fargo not been holding him. "Try to walk," Fargo said, and the man moaned in agony as he put one foot forward. He slid his other foot forward, his body trembling as Fargo helped him. Then, with a shuddering groan, he slid from Fargo's grip and collapsed on the floor. Fargo knelt on one knee beside him for a moment, pressed one hand to the side of the man's neck, and finally rose to his feet. The coachman had taken his final step.

Fargo left the house. Others would come looking for Ryan and find him, and he had no time to go back to Eugene now. He swung onto the Ovaro and set out to the shore of the winding ribbon that was the Willamette River. Some of the pieces had come together. The coach driver had been paid well to do what he was told with no questions asked: first to be part of the deception and wander the hills, then to return and take Galina away. But they had returned and killed him. The old truth that dead men won't talk. It had almost worked twice, Fargo thought grimly, and kept the Ovaro at a trot as he rode along the river's right bank. The day drifted into dusk and he had passed a half-dozen houses, some on his side of the river, some on the far side. But all were weathered frame structures of gray or dirty white.

He slowed but kept riding as night fell, passing two more houses that took form in the moonlight, neither fitting the description the coachman had muttered. He had gone on for another hour when a structure took shape ahead of him, a light in two of the windows, and he slowed the Ovaro to a walk. Drawing closer, he half-smiled in satisfaction as he saw the red bricks of the house. Dismounting, he walked closer to the house, halting to tether the horse to the end of a low branch before moving closer in a crouching lope. He dropped to one knee at the window and peered over the sill to see two men and Galina. One was the red-bearded Krasnow, the other one of his American hirelings. Galina sat in a straight-backed chair, hands bound in front of her. She wore only a slip, and her shoulders, arms, and back were red with bruises and welts where she'd been beaten. The window was open six inches at the bottom, allowing him to hear as well as see.

"She took more than I figured she would," Fargo heard the American say.

"Galina is a very, how you say, *tough* young woman. She has always been made of steel," Krasnow said, and with one hand lifted Galina's chin up. "As befits her position, isn't that so, my lovely?" he said. "A member of the czar's inner family."

Galina spat at him in Russian, and Fargo didn't need a translation to understand her reply. Krasnow's face froze and he slapped her across the cheek. Galina refused to flinch and cursed again at him in Russian.

The American leaned against a wall. "How long before your friend gets here with this Pavlev guy?" he asked.

"Not before morning, I'd say," Krasnow answered.

"What do you think he'll do with her?" the man questioned.

"I know exactly what he'll do. Pavlev is a very smart man. When he hears we have convinced her to tell us where her father is, he'll send me to Rhesnev with an offer. It will be a trade-off, as you Americans say. He calls off the search and leaves for Russia and he gets his daughter back. If not, she is dead," Krasnow said and turned to Galina, who watched him with her brown eyes narrowed. "You or the czar, my dear. That will be his choice," he said and turned back to the American. "Which do you think he'll take?" Krasnow asked.

"Jesus, his daughter, naturally," the man said.

Krasnow's slow smile was laced with ice. "You'll notice the lovely Galina has not answered," he said, and Fargo, staring through the window at Galina, saw her face remain impassive. "She is not so confident as you are, my friend," Krasnow said to his hired hand. Again,

Galina stayed silent, her face a lovely mask. Krasnow was right. Galina was not certain of the choice her father would make, Fargo realized with a sense of shock. He was still turning the astonishing thought over in his mind when Krasnow supplied perhaps part of the reason. "Tell our American friend here about choices, my dear Galina," Krasnow said.

"He's not my American friend. You tell him whatever you like, pig," Galina spat back.

"What did you tell that oaf we killed? You probably told him you came to help your father recover the egg," Krasnow said to Galina. Again she refused to answer, and he laughed and rubbed a hand across her right breast. "Of course that's what you did. That was far easier than having to explain that your father came along to help you. And the oaf believed it, naturally." Galina's eyes were shooting daggers at Krasnow as he turned away.

Fargo felt his initial sense of shock turning to anger. Lovely Galina had apparently been less than truthful with him, and he wanted to find out more. But Krasnow and the gunhand stood in the way. He'd have to tend to them first, and he scanned the room again. It was small, too small to burst in and risk a shoot-out where wild bullets could hit Galina as she sat immobile in the chair. He'd have to draw at least one of them outside. He reached down to the calf holster around his leg and pulled out the thin, double-edged throwing knife, a perfectly balanced example of the forger's art. He saw a narrow length of branch lying on the ground, picked it up, and sent it skittering across the bottom of the closed door. Inside the room, the two men spun as one. "What was that?" Krasnow barked.

"I don't know. Maybe a coon or a fox, they come close to a house," the American said.

"Go and see," Krasnow ordered, and Fargo moved from the windowsill as the American started for the door, drawing his six-gun as he did. Ducking around the corner of the house, Fargo dropped to his stomach in the deepest shadows, the throwing knife in the palm of his hand. An oblong rectangle of light followed the man outside as he stepped from the house, peered into the darkness, then moved out of the square of light. Fargo saw him glance at the length of branch, ignore it, then move closer, his revolver raised and ready to fire. Fargo rose to his knees and flung the slender knife with a swift, underhand motion, the blade hurtling silently through the night.

The man never saw the steel death, hardly felt it pierce through the base of his neck. But he did feel the instant anguish of sudden death as his trachea was pierced. He staggered three steps forward and managed to pull the blade from his throat before he collapsed facedown on the ground. Fargo ran forward, retrieved the blade, wiped it clean on the back of the man's shirt, and flattened himself against the bricks of the house, less than a foot from the window. "You see anything?" Krasnow called from inside the house and waited for the answer that would not come. "You out there?" the Russian called again. Again silence was his only answer, and Fargo heard a curse in Russian as he dropped to one knee to peer over the windowsill. Krasnow had a revolver in hand, a heavy Russian *Tula,* and he had circled behind Galina and held the gun against the back of her neck. He spoke in Russian to her but she answered in English.

"Something is wrong? Yes, it would seem so," she said, icy pleasure in her voice. Krasnow kept the revolver on her as he called out again.

"Who is out there?"

Fargo, staying low, edged toward the open doorway. "It's the oaf you killed. Surprise," he said.

"Fargo," Galina gasped out, a half laugh of triumph in her voice.

"Dmitri didn't do his job," Krasnow said.

"He tried," Fargo said. "I'm hard to kill."

"Come to the door with your hands up," the Russian ordered. "Do it or I kill her."

"Pavlev won't like that. He'll want to question her. Besides, she could be his bargaining card with Rhesnev. You said so yourself," Fargo returned.

Krasnow hesitated, but only for a moment. "Pavlev will understand what I had to do," he said. "And I will kill her unless you come out with your hands up."

Fargo swore silently as he heard the agitation in the Russian's voice. The man was on the edge—nervous, fearful, and determined to salvage some form of victory. Galina was closer to death than she realized. Or perhaps she did realize it, Fargo reflected. She was being completely quiet, saying nothing to push Krasnow over the edge. He'd have to do the same, Fargo realized—stick his neck out and hope for the split second he would need. Reaching down, he drew the throwing knife from its calf holster once more and pushed the blade up into the sleeve of his right arm. Holstering the Colt, he raised his arms into the air and stepped into the doorway, his eyes on Galina at once. She sat quietly, Krasnow still holding the heavy pistol to her neck.

"Step inside more," Krasnow ordered, and Fargo obeyed, keeping his arms raised. "Drop your gunbelt," the Russian said. "Slowly." Fargo lowered his arms, using his left hand to undo the buckle of the gunbelt. The belt fell to his feet. "Kick it away from you," Krasnow said and again Fargo obeyed, the throwing knife still inside the sleeve of his shirt. He kept it in place by pressing his arm against his side. Krasnow pulled the pistol from Galina's neck but still held it alongside her face. His eyes were narrowed on the big man in front of him. "Dmitri was sure he had killed you," he said.

"Everybody's entitled to one mistake," Fargo said with a half shrug. "Where is he now?"

"He went to get Pavlev," Krasnow said.

"So we just wait," Fargo said.

"That's right. You can wait alive or you can wait dead," Krasnow growled. "That's up to you."

"I'll wait alive," Fargo said.

"Then get over here with her so I can keep an eye on the two of you at once," Krasnow said and stepped away from Galina. He felt in charge again, Fargo saw, some of his nervousness gone and his reflexes relaxed just enough. Fargo moved slowly toward Galina. As he did so he moved his right arm from against his side, an imperceptible movement but enough to let the thin blade drop into his palm. Krasnow snapped something to Galina in Russian and she hissed her reply. Fargo saw Krasnow's eyes leave him for a moment to glance at Galina. With a flick of his wrist, Fargo hurled the throwing knife across the short distance. Krasnow, suddenly aware of movement, turned as the knife ripped through his hand.

He cursed in pain, his fingers reflexively tightening on the trigger. His shot went wild. The knife was still in his hand as he tried to bring the gun around and fire again, but Fargo was at him, slamming his fist onto the hilt of the knife. Krasnow howled in pain as the knife cut downward and the gun fell from his fingers. Fargo's short left hook caught him on the point of the jaw, the red beard absorbing some of the blow, but the Russian went down nonetheless. As he lay on his back, blinking, Fargo pulled the knife from his hand and scooped up the revolver. Krasnow needed another few seconds to fully regain consciousness, and Fargo used the time to cut Galina's wrist ropes. She leaped to her feet, arms encircling him.

"Later, honey," he said and watched Krasnow sit up.

"Kill him," Galina said, staring at Krasnow.

"Not so fast," Fargo said as Krasnow glared up at him and held his hand to his chest.

"My hand needs bandaging," he said.

"In time," Fargo said and handed the pistol to Galina. "Pavlev might get back early. I want to put my horse out of sight," he told her. "Keep him covered. Don't shoot unless he tries to get away. I've a few things to ask him." His eyes went to the man. "Don't do anything stupid. She knows how to shoot," he said.

"I'm sure," Krasnow grunted, and Fargo strode from the house. Outside, he hurried to where he had tethered the Ovaro and moved the horse deeper into the quaking aspen, until the animal was completely out of sight in a dense thicket. He had just finished giving the horse a comfortably long tether when the shot shattered the night.

"Shit," Fargo swore as he spun and raced through the trees and back to the house, the Colt in his hand. He slowed when he passed the window and glimpsed Galina standing, the heavy Russian revolver in her hand. He stepped through the doorway and saw Krasnow on the floor, his red beard stained a new shade that matched the stain on his face and neck.

"He jumped at me, tried to pull the gun away from me. I had to shoot," Galina said. "Get him out of here, please. It's so horrible." Fargo took the man's arms and dragged his lifeless body from the house, across the ground, and deposited his grisly burden in the trees behind the house. He returned to see Galina slumped in a chair where she had drawn a blouse around her torn slip. She had put the pistol on the small table, and her brown eyes were deep with swirling emotions as she watched him enter. "I'll go and change," she said, gesturing to an adjoining room. "When they took me from the hotel, they also took my bags and my horse. No traces left that way."

"Let's talk first," Fargo said.

"Talk?" Galina inquired.

"It seems you haven't exactly been giving me the truth, from what I heard Krasnow say. I wanted to ask him more about that. Now I'm asking you," Fargo said.

Galina gave a little half shrug. "What you heard is true. I am not here to help my father. He is here to help me. You see, the egg was in my trust when it was stolen. Gustave Fabergé was to come to cement three of the pearls that had come loose. You would have to know my country and the way things are done by the czar to understand what it meant to have the egg stolen from my trust."

"I'd guess he wasn't happy with you," Fargo said.

"I would have been punished, at least banned from the czar's palace circle. But my father, being one of Czar Alexander's advisors, convinced him to let me try to recover the egg and to let him go along."

"Why didn't you just say that?" Fargo queried.

Galina shrugged again. "We thought it seemed simpler to say I was helping Nicholas."

Fargo turned the answer over in his mind. It was reasonable enough on the surface, yet an insistent nagging stayed inside him. "How much else seemed simpler to leave out?" he pressed.

"Nothing. We just didn't think Americans would understand how things are done in Russia, and we couldn't really explain. The czar is a just and honorable man, but my failure reflected on my entire family. It is our way.

The czar must set an example in his Imperial circle for everyone," Galina said. Again, her explanations were reasonable and Fargo decided he'd no excuse not to accept them, so he ignored the inner nagging that refused to go away. "Will I be the bait again when Pavlev arrives?" she asked, cutting into his thoughts.

"No. Your countrymen are too good at this kind of thing. It went wrong last time. I don't want that to happen again. In fact, I'm thinking this is a job I should finish alone," Fargo said.

"But I'm here now. Make use of me," Galina insisted.

"Yes, but not that way. I'll make use of your shooting skills. Finish dressing. We're going to wait in the trees," he told her, and Galina went into the other room, returning with her blouse neatly tucked into a black skirt. "You take that pistol. You're familiar with it," he said and turned the lamp down low. Galina picked up the pistol and followed him outside, where he went into the trees and found a good soft patch of fescue grass amid the maples. He settled down on it where he could see every approach to the house.

"I expect the one that went to fetch Pavlev will return with him," Galina said as she sat down close to Fargo. "We'll take them when they reach the house?"

"I'll take Pavlev. I want him alive to answer questions," Fargo said.

"Be careful with Pavlev. He is the brains behind everything."

"Then he'll know where the egg is," Fargo said.

"I should expect so. But he is a dangerous man," Galina said.

"I'm sure of that," Fargo said, then felt Galina's warm softness come against him and her lips were on his, parting, lingering, finally pulling back. "We can't. I want to be ready if they come back early," Fargo said.

"I know. Just a reminder," Galina murmured and moved away. He heard her lie down on the grass in the blackness of the woods and he stretched out beside her. He let his eyes close as he relaxed, focusing his hearing on the night sounds of the woods. They had outfoxed him once. He wasn't about to let it happen again. He made it a practice not to underestimate anyone, and he had violated that practice once. He wouldn't do it twice. Pavlev wouldn't come riding up to the house, Fargo wagered. He was far too experienced in the ways of intrigue for that. But whatever the Russian did, Fargo knew he had to be ready to react quickly, and he lay silently, letting his ears become the total focus of all his senses.

5

The night seemed to be endless as he lay unmoving and heard the sound of Galina's steady breathing. She had fallen asleep. He smiled to himself. She was still asleep when the first tentative fingers of gray light pushed into the woods. Fargo remained motionless, his ears taking in the sounds of the morning birds, picking out the goldfinch, Bullock's oriole, and yellow warbler. It was a nice sound. He listened as suddenly the sound grew different, louder, more agitated, and his eyes snapped open. The birds were winging off in different directions. They had been disturbed. Now he strained his ears.

The other sound drifted to his ear, the faint, rustling sound of leaves rubbing against each other. Something or someone moved through the woods, not more than twenty yards away. Fargo sat up and placed one hand over Galina's mouth. Her eyes came open, fear flashing in them for an instant until she saw his face. He took his hand away, put one finger to his lips, and she nodded as she sat up. He swung onto one knee and peered through the trees, Galina against him. The figure finally appeared, on foot, moving carefully from the edge of the trees. Fargo recognized the man's face at once. He had only glimpsed it for a fleeting instant inside a sack, but it was an instant forever engraved in his mind. The man advanced on the house in the early morning light, and Fargo put his lips to Galina's ear, his voice a barely audible whisper.

"Pavlev's here, being real careful. He's got Dmitri out front for him. When Dmitri reaches the house, he'll signal for Pavlev to come forward or stay back. We let him do it. You cover him, but don't do anything unless he runs from the house. Then bring him down, understand?"

Galina turned her face, and he felt her lips against his ear. "Where will you be?" she whispered.

"Going after Pavlev," he said and rose to one knee as Dmitri neared the house. The man had come from the woods to his left. Squeezing Galina's shoulder for a moment, Fargo moved away. On steps silent as a panther's, he made his way through the trees in a low crouch as his eyes swept the thick foliage. Nothing moved, and he glanced toward the house to see Dmitri going through the open doorway. He reappeared in an instant to stand in the doorway and wave both arms frantically.

Fargo's eyes returned to the trees and he saw the low branches move, some twenty-five yards to his right. No faint sound this time, but the brush of leaves being pushed away hard. Pavlev was racing away, running for a horse he'd left back further. Fargo frowned and silently swore. He was too far from the Ovaro to reach it in time, and he rose and crashed through the trees as he followed the sound of Pavlev's flight. He suddenly caught a glimpse of the man as the Russian turned, glancing back as he heard the sound of pursuit. Fargo saw a gaunt face, younger than he'd expected, with heavy eyebrows. A pistol was clutched in his right hand. Spinning, Pavlev raced away again as Fargo ran after him, closing the distance between them. Suddenly the man veered to the right, then the left. Fargo followed and saw him dart behind the wide trunk of an aspen. Fargo drew his Colt as he slowed, edged forward, and halted behind a tree of his own.

As he waited, a frown touched his forehead. There'd been no shot from Galina. Maybe Dmitri had retreated back into the house and she was still watching and waiting. But he couldn't concern himself with that now, he knew. He had to concentrate on Pavlev, and as that thought sank into him, he heard a sound from behind the tree. The Russian was running again, moving straight through the forest, and Fargo spun around the tree trunk, glimpsed the fleeing figure, and gave chase again. He was closing distance when the shot exploded. But it was not the shot from Galina. This shot tore through the shoulder of his shirt and sent a spray of wood chips into his face from where the bullet slammed into the tree he was passing.

He fell forward as he cursed under his breath. They had outsmarted him again. Pavlev had sent Dmitri as his front man, then ran at the signal that something was wrong. But all the while he'd had a third man lying in wait. The Russian was a master of intrigue and plotting. Now Fargo didn't move, the Colt in his hand concealed by his body. He had pitched forward. Anyone watching would think the shot got him, and he continued to lie motionless on the ground. He guessed perhaps thirty seconds had passed when he heard the footsteps nearing—careful, cautious steps. He heard one pair, then a second pair of footsteps coming up. The first set came to a halt at his side, and the toe of a boot dug into the space between his ribs and the ground and he was lifted and turned onto his back. As he rolled and his back touched the ground, through eyes that were slitted closed, he could make out the bulk of the figure. His finger tightened on the trigger, squeezed off two shots, and his eyes snapped open to see the man catapult backwards with his abdomen streaming red.

Fargo rolled and the shot thudded into the ground where he had been. He saw Pavlev a dozen feet away. He rolled again as he fired, saw Pavlev twist away, turn to run, and Fargo's Colt fired another shot. Pavlev grunted in pain as he stumbled forward and fell, clutching at his leg. Fargo, staying on his stomach, fired again as Pavlev tried to get up and run on. This time the Russian half-screamed in pain as the shot landed in the same spot as the last one. He fell forward, cursing in Russian, dragged himself half around, and raised the pistol to fire. Fargo's shot blew the pistol from the man's hand and Pavlev fell backwards with a curse of pain.

Fargo rose to his feet and stepped to where Pavlev half-lay, half-sat, deep, dark eyes burning at him from his gaunt face. "Not last time and not this time either, mister," Fargo said. "Close but no cigar." He holstered the Colt and stared down at the Russian. "Give me answers and you stay alive," he said.

Pavlev winced in pain as he tried to move his leg, and his dark eyes shot hatred up at the big man in front of him. "You won't get your hands on it. Others have it, in a safe place. Kill me, if you want," he said.

Fargo frowned down at the man, the answer hanging in his mind. It was the kind of selflessness he'd never found among thieves. Maybe Russian thieves were different than the homegrown ones? he wondered. "You'd do that?" he asked. "Die so the others could get the money?"

"What money?" the Russian asked through his pain.

"The money you'll get for the egg. That's why you stole it," Fargo said.

"Is that what they told you?" Pavlev sneered.

"Yes," Fargo nodded.

"Clever," Pavlev grunted.

"You saying the egg isn't worth a lot of money?" Fargo frowned.

"Oh, it is worth a lot of money," Pavlev said. "But do you really think the czar of all the Russias, one of the richest rulers in the world, would care this much about one jeweled egg, no matter how much it was worth?"

Fargo frowned as he considered the reproof in the question. "All right, maybe it's not what it's worth that's important to him. Maybe it's getting back what was stolen. I've seen a horse thief chased across the country and killed, not because the horse was so valuable but because the owner wouldn't sit still for being robbed. A lot of people are like that. Maybe the czar is one of them."

The Russian gave a derisive hoot. "You Americans are so concerned with money and so naive. The Rhesnev's concocted their story well."

"This American's been paid to do a job, and he's going to do it. Where's the goddamn egg?" Fargo bit out.

"You'll never find it. Kill me if you want," Pavlev said, and Fargo swore inwardly. The man didn't seem to be uttering empty challenges. Yet maybe he was a good actor.

"If you think I wouldn't, you're making a damn big mistake, mister," Fargo said. The Russian shrugged but said nothing. "I'm going to give you a little time to think about whether your life's worth it," Fargo said. "Where's your damn horse?" Pavlev gestured toward the maples at his back. "Start crawling," Fargo snapped.

"I can't, not with my leg. The bone is shattered," Pavlev said. "Bring the horse here. You can help me on."

"Meanwhile, you crawl away," Fargo said. "No thanks."

"How far do you think I could crawl with this leg?" Pavlev asked with practical logic.

Fargo's eyes peered at the man. His answer had been realistic. He wouldn't go far, and any trail he'd leave would be child's play to follow. "All right, I'll bring the horse," Fargo said. "Meanwhile, you'd better start thinking about how much staying alive is worth. I could run out of patience at any time."

The Russian lay back with a sigh of something that sounded like a combination of relief and pain. Fargo picked up the Russian revolver, pushed it into the waistband of his trousers, and hurried through the woods. He heard the horse after a few minutes, moving against low branches, and found the animal tied on a long tether. He led the horse back to find Pavlev had managed to drag himself to a tree, where he sat with his back against the trunk. Pavlev's right hand lay hardly visible against his far side, and as Fargo approached, his eyes were on the man's face. When he saw Pavlev's mouth tighten in a moment of pain, he flung himself in a headlong dive sideways. He only had time to glimpse the Russian's hand come up with the small pistol in it as the shot rang out, the bullet passing just behind his diving body.

Fargo hit the ground as a second bullet whizzed by a fraction of an inch from his cheek, and he drew the Colt as he rolled, came up against a tree trunk, and fired off three shots, each of them hurtling into the form against the tree trunk. Pavlev's body bucked for a moment and then went limp. Fargo saw the gun fall from the man's hand as his arm fell to his side. "Dammit," Fargo swore as he rose and walked toward the lifeless form and the small pistol on the ground beside it, a Russian version of a Starr four-barreled derringer with rifled steel barrels for rimfire cartridges.

He wanted to go through Pavlev's clothes but that could wait. The man wasn't going anywhere. Fargo dropped the horse's reins over a low branch and began to make his way back to where he had left Galina. There had still been no shot from Galina and a worried frown dug into his brow as he wondered what that meant. Moving in a low crouch, he slowed when he neared the house and went forward on slow, stealthy steps until he saw Galina, still crouched, watching the house. She turned when he came up to her and her arms were around him instantly. "My God, you are alive. I heard the shooting and I was afraid," she said.

"Pavlev had a friend waiting. They're both dead now," Fargo said.

"Did you find out where the egg is?" Galina asked.

"No, dammit," Fargo bit out, then his eyes went to the house. "He still in there?"

"Yes."

"You sure?" Fargo questioned.

"He hasn't come out," Galina said, and Fargo swore under his breath.

"There's a back room and probably a window," he rasped, and Galina gave a tiny gasp of dismay.

"You keep covering the door," Fargo said and left her in a low, crouching lope as he moved along to the side of the house, stayed in the trees until he reached the rear, and then darted into the open. He halted against the house, along the rear wall, edged his way around the corner, and swore again. There was no rear window. He rose, keeping against the outer wall of the house until he reached the front door, where he paused, listening. He heard nothing from inside the house. Galina watched from the trees, he knew, and he dropped to his stomach and began to crawl through the doorway.

He halted at once as he saw the body facedown on the floor. He rose to his feet and stepped inside the house to see the spreading red stains that came from both of the man's wrists, the knife on the floor nearby. Dmitri had slit his wrists. The frown was deep on Fargo's brow as he went to the door and beckoned to Galina. He was standing inside the house, staring down at the man as Galina came in. "He killed himself," she remarked, staring at the figure.

"You don't seem surprised," Fargo said with a frown.

"Should I be? Isn't that what criminals do?" she asked, and Fargo's frown deepened.

"Rejected lovers kill themselves. So do disgraced statesmen, dishonored leaders, and idealists who'd rather die than betray a cause. Ordinary thieves fight, run, or give up. They never confuse money with honor," he said.

"I guess these are not ordinary thieves," Galina said, dismissing the subject.

"Pavlev was willing to cash it in, too. Something doesn't fit right," Fargo muttered. "He sounded as though they didn't steal the egg for the money they'd get selling it. He as much as said that wasn't why you and your father were chasing them."

"Of course he'd say something like that. Thieves don't tell the truth," Galina answered, imperious dismissal still in her answers. Fargo fell silent as he walked from the house. Galina followed him. He felt dissatisfied and uneasy. She had already given him one story that she admitted wasn't the truth. Had she given him another that was less than the whole truth? Yet he hadn't any proof of that, either. All he had was formless misgivings, but they still added up to something that didn't fit right. Pavlev's sneering questions, his implications, and his willingness to sacrifice himself, along with Dmitri's suicide, were all part of what refused to fit. These things weren't explained away by Galina's imperious dismissals.

He peered at her as she halted beside him, her hand sliding into his and her deep brown eyes searching his face. Perhaps she didn't know the whole truth, either, he pondered. Or perhaps he just didn't want to believe otherwise of her. That was all too possible, he realized. "What now?" she asked.

"Pavlev left a trail somewhere. I'll find it," Fargo said. "Alone." Galina's blond eyebrows lifted and he saw protest form in her face. "These boys, for whatever their reasons, are playing for keeps. They almost killed you once. My fault. I underestimated them. I don't want you to pay for another mistake. I'm going it on my own."

"No, you'll need me," she said.

"I'll make do," he said.

"My father would never forgive me if I didn't go with you," she said.

"You tell him you didn't have a choice," he said.

"Is that what you're telling me?" Galina asked gravely.

"It is," he said. She accepted defeat with a glare. "You can find your way back to your father," he said and handed her Pavlev's pistol. "You've your own gun. Now you've another," he said. She put the pistol in her waistband, then took his hand and thrust it into her blouse. His fingers curled over the warm, soft breast.

"Take me with you. We won't find the egg tomorrow. We'll have time for each other," Galina said. "I want you, Fargo."

"Good try but no sale," Fargo said as he drew his hand back.

She offered a half pout that didn't really fit the cool, high-cheekboned beauty of her. "You've forgotten so quickly," she said.

"Haven't forgotten anything. That's why I want you waiting in one piece when I get back," he told her. She continued to pout but her eyes softened. "Get your things and your horse," he said gruffly and went outside. She returned in the saddle, her eyes studying him.

"Be very careful with it if you find it. It would not do to have it destroyed after all the trouble we've gone to to get it back," Galina said.

"I'll wrap it in cotton," Fargo said and watched her ride away, her back straight, a regality to her bearing. She had become a beautiful question mark. Or, more accurately, she had suddenly become surrounded by questions that defied her simple, dismissive answers. When she was out of sight, he walked back to where he had left Pavlev. He knelt beside the body, went through the man's clothes, and found nothing to help him. Next he examined the man's boots and felt a frown touch his brow.

A dusting of small, yellow-white flecks formed a line inside the cracks and crinkles of the man's boots, some stuck into the sides of his soles. The small flecks came loose as he ran his finger across them. The frown on his brow grew deeper as he rubbed the little flecks in his fingers. "Sawdust," he muttered aloud and pushed to his feet to go over to the man's horse. He lifted the horse's left forefoot and examined the hoof. The encrusted bits of dirt were ordinary enough, he noted—no red clay, no black loam, heavy sand, bits of thick riverbank soil, nothing that would offer a clue to where the horse had been. But his eyes narrowed as he spied the yellow-white flecks caught around the nailheads in the hoof and wedged into the edges of the shoe and the calkin.

He examined the other three shoes and saw they all carried little pieces of sawdust. He stared into space after he put the last foot down. The man had been someplace where there was sawdust. But the horse too? Fargo grimaced at the question. He could understand the sawdust on the man's boots. Many saloons had sawdust-covered floors. But the horse hadn't been in saloons. And stables often used straw on their floors but not sawdust. The Russian had left him with one more question, this one not of words but of substance. Fargo walked to where he had left the Ovaro, swung onto the horse, and collected Pavlev's mount. He'd rid himself of the horse and saddle at the first town. He slowly walked the Ovaro through the forest in the direction the Russian had come. He crisscrossed the forest and finally picked up the trail—two horses moving through the woods, then separating.

He followed the trail backwards to where Pavlev and his man had entered the forest from a narrow road, then tracked the prints south where they turned to border the Cascade Range. The edge of the Cascade Range looked down on a line of towns, well separated from each other but all with one thing in common—all had grown from logging stations. As he rode, Pavlev's trail disappeared in an area of soft earth too well crossed with heavy wagon tracks.

It was late afternoon when Fargo reached the first town. He sold the horse and saddle at the local smithy's place and went on to stop at the general store first, then the stable, and finally the saloon. It was a routine he followed at every town he visited, and his question was the same for every blacksmith, storekeeper, stableman, and bartender: "You see a tall foreigner with sunken cheeks and a Russian accent?" The merchants all said they hadn't seen such a man and the barkeeps embellished their answers a little: "I'd remember somebody like that drinking at my bar."

The stables all had straw on their floors, and most of the saloons had sawdust sprinkled on their floors. Fargo decided against asking if they'd had any horses in their saloons, and he was beginning to feel the first stabs of discouragement when he reached a little town that had named itself Bucksaw after its logging heritage. It was only when he reached the saloon that he felt the excitement stab at him. "Yeah, Russian dude. I saw him around. There were three of them," the bartender said. Fargo accounted for two silently—Pavlev and Dmitri. "But they never came in here, none of them," the man added, and Fargo swore inwardly. That meant the sawdust on Pavlev's boots had come from somewhere else. But he had at least picked up a trail point. Pavlev had been here. He had started to turn away when the bartender spoke up again. "You want this Russian, you ought to see Sheriff MacCauley," he said.

"Why?" Fargo asked.

"The sheriff was after him when he took off," the barkeep said. "Sheriff's office is in the center of town."

"Much obliged," Fargo said and hurried from the saloon. He walked his horse down the main street of town and found the sheriff's office, the man inside wearing a large star on a cloth vest. Square-faced, graying, but with shrewd, appraising gray eyes, the sheriff watched him enter. "Name's Fargo, Sheriff. The bartender at the saloon said I ought to pay you a visit."

"About what, Fargo?" the sheriff said.

"I've been trailing a Russian named Pavlev." Sheriff MacCauley's brows lifted.

"You a marshal?" the sheriff asked.

"No, working for someone who wants this man," Fargo said. "What can you tell me about him?"

"Not much. He was living in the Sinclairs' barn with

two of his friends; paid a month's rent though he only stayed ten days."

"I understand you want him, too. Why?" Fargo asked.

"He damn near killed one of his friends right in front of me, then hightailed it out of here with the other," the sheriff said. "His friend was lucky; the three bullets all passed through his side. All he's got is a couple of broken ribs. I'm holding him in the cell back of us."

"Why you holding him?" Fargo frowned.

"Bait. I'm betting this Pavlev's coming back to finish the job. There's something personal I don't know about in it. This Pavlev called the guy he shot a name before he shot him," Sheriff MacCauley said.

"Pavlev's not coming back. He's dead," Fargo said.

"You sure about that?" the sheriff frowned.

"I ought to know. I killed him," Fargo said, and the sheriff's brows lifted.

"What the hell is all this about? What are these Russians doing around here?" MacCauley questioned. Fargo decided that the less he explained the better it'd be.

"I don't know for sure," he said, and the answer wasn't really a lie. "But there's no point in holding onto the man you have now," Fargo remarked, plans quickly forming inside his mind.

"I guess not," the sheriff said.

"Do me a favor. Turn him over to me. He might be of value to me if I handle it right," Fargo said.

"That's fine with me," the sheriff shrugged.

"But I want to look around that barn they were living in first," Fargo said.

"Take the road south out of town. You'll see it, maybe a mile or so out, tall barn with a hole in one part of the roof," the sheriff said.

"I'll be back," Fargo said as he hurried from the office.

He found the barn and stepped inside it and surveyed the residue of primitive living—clothes still strewn about, dishes still encrusted with food, blankets strewn over cots. He examined the inside of the barn carefully, and under one of the cots he found tiny pieces of the sawdust. They had been brought in on boots, probably Pavlev's. There was no sawdust anywhere else in the barn, the flooring covered with dust and nothing more. Nor were there any notes or markings to help him. Only one thing had become clear. The sawdust still remained his only trail, and it was the most tenuous trail he'd ever followed.

The day had begun to draw to a close when he arrived back at the sheriff's office. "Find anything?" MacCauley asked.

"No," Fargo said. "I'll take the Russian off your hands."

"He's all yours," the sheriff said and unlocked the cell door. Fargo stepped in to see a thin man with a black beard and eyes that could only be called sad.

"What's your name?" Fargo asked him.

"Boris," the man muttered.

"I can help you," Fargo said, and Boris looked up at him with a frown of appraisal that somehow didn't affect the sad, deep eyes.

"Why?" he asked.

"I want some answers from you," Fargo said.

"Who are you?" the man queried.

"That's not important. I can save you from Pavlev," Fargo said and saw an instant of hope flicker in the man's eyes. "But I'll do it only if I get answers from you."

"Not here. Get me out of here," Boris said.

"Let's go," Fargo said, and the man picked up a small sack from the cot and hurried from the cell after Fargo. "Obliged," Fargo nodded to the sheriff as he left. He paused outside to survey the Russian. "You have a horse?" he asked.

"Not anymore," the man said.

"Then you'll walk for now," Fargo said and swung onto the pinto. The man walked in silence beside him as Fargo led the way out of town and along the road as night fell. Leaving the road, Fargo moved up a gentle slope to a stand of white fir where he halted and dismounted. The Russian watched him with nervousness and suspicion on his face.

"Why are you helping me?" he questioned.

"Do you know where the egg is, Boris?" Fargo returned, ignoring the man's question. He saw Boris's eyes grow wide.

"No. You are after the egg?" Boris said. "You must be with them."

"With who?" Fargo queried.

"The ones the czar sent after us," Boris said.

"Guess so," Fargo said. "Where is the egg?"

"I said, I don't know."

"You were with Pavlev and you don't know?" Fargo pressed.

"He didn't tell us everything," the man said. "I took orders from him. We all did. But he didn't tell us much."

"Why did Pavlev try to kill you?" Fargo questioned.

"Because he is a madman," Boris said.

He *was,* Fargo corrected silently. "What did he call you? The sheriff said he called you a name." Fargo pressed, trying to work around the man's reluctant evasiveness.

"A traitor," Boris said, his deep eyes filling with pain.

"Why did he call you a traitor?" Fargo asked and saw the Russian's eyes grow cautiously uncomfortable as he searched for an answer.

"I wanted to go home. I didn't want any more. I never cared like the others," Boris said.

"Cared about what?" Fargo pursued.

The man grew more wary, his sad eyes looking away. "Nothing. It is nothing. I've no more to tell you. I want to leave, leave here, leave you, leave this country."

Traitor. Fargo turned the word over in his mind. He had seen thieves that backed out of a gang. Sometimes they were shot. At best they were called gutless cowards, fools, and a dozen other epithets. But never traitors. Getting cold feet didn't make a traitor. You had to have a cause, a principle, an ideal, to be a traitor. The word echoed Dmitri's suicide. It hinted at more then mere money, more than a robbery, even a very big one. "You haven't given me enough answers," Fargo said.

"I say no more," Boris returned.

"Where were you going to sell the egg?" Fargo asked.

"I know nothing about that," the man said.

"Somebody knew," Fargo pressed.

"Pavlev, maybe a few others. I don't know," Boris insisted. "I have nothing more to say. I am going."

"I can make you tell me more," Fargo growled, but he saw no fear come into the man's eyes. Instead, the sadness in them only grew deeper.

"No, you cannot. You can kill me. I think you will do a better job of that than Pavlev did," the man said.

"You can be damn sure of that," Fargo said, and his hand went to the butt of his Colt.

But the man only shrugged. "In my country, we learn to be fatalists. It is the armor of the little people. Do what you want. I am going," he said, then rose to his feet and picked up his sack as he started to walk away.

Fargo cursed silently. Convinced that Boris didn't have the important answers, Fargo watched him fade away in the night and knew he had been defeated in a way he'd never been before. The man had simply ceased to care and so he was beyond reaching. Fargo turned away, took a blanket from his saddlebag, and lay down. Come morning, he'd set out again on the sawdust trail, the strangest trail he had ever followed. But that seemed only fitting. Chasing a jeweled Easter egg was one of the strangest tasks he'd ever taken on.

6

Two more days had gone by and two more towns. On the third day Fargo began to wonder if he searched in the wrong direction. He'd followed southward, in the direction Pavlev had arrived from, but perhaps the man had veered east or west. He pondered the thought as he came to still another town in the midafternoon. It had more substance than the others, he saw at once, and noted a dozen well-tended houses on the outskirts. Once in the town, he saw wagons loaded with sheep wool, which attested to sheep farms in the area, plus a good sprinkling of fruit rack and grocery wagons, as well as heavier Owensboro freight rigs. He passed a barber shop, a small church, and a bank, all marks of a town with roots. He noted the name on the bank: Goverstown Trust Co.

Women with youngsters in family spring wagons also attested to the town's stability, he noted as he rode slowly down the wide main street to come to a halt at the general store. As he dismounted, he noted the large, colorful poster in the store window and paused to read it. The words KELLY'S CIRCUS headlined the poster, over drawings of elephants, tigers, acrobats, a fire-eating sword-swallower, and clowns. "See Ahmed from Calcutta, he walks on fire and swallows swords," the copy on the placard read. "See the three Risselli brothers, acrobats extraordinary from Italy; Rudy from Vienna and his fierce tigers; the high-flying, death-defying aerialist, Tanya of Moscow; and the greatest clowns in any circus. See all this and more. Performances every night. Two weeks only. Come one and all."

He was frowning at the poster, Fargo realized, his eyes focused on the words "Tanya of Moscow." But it was something else that exploded within him, something not on the poster. Circus rings were covered with sawdust. Sawdust was a part of circuses. The fact seized him. Sawdust and Tanya of Moscow. It was too much of a coincidence. He had found the end of the sawdust trail, he thought silently. Turning away from the window, he led the Ovaro down the street to the edge of town, where he found the circus tents, the main one large and striped yellow and blue. Four smaller tents surrounded it, and in a half circle were an assortment of circus wagons, some brilliantly painted. Those were living-quarter wagons and the barred wagons that contained a half-dozen pacing tigers. The big dead-axle drays were without the garish circus colors and were used for transporting the tents, posts, and other heavy equipment. He noted six elephants being fed off to one side, and nearby the closed, high wagon that was plainly the office and owner's quarters.

He moved closer to where three acrobats were practicing and a young woman in a ballerina tutu executed pirouettes to the accompaniment of a man playing an upright piano. A pair of clowns, without facial makeup but in their baggy pants and oversize shoes, experimented with new routines. He felt the Ovaro shy as he passed a wagon holding a pacing tiger, and he moved away and reached the main tent, where he stepped inside and his eyes moved around the huge circular ring, which was covered with sawdust. This was where Pavlev had picked up the sawdust on his boots and on his horse's hooves, Fargo muttered again to himself. He knew he had to form plans quickly, but he also knew one other thing—he had to move carefully and cleverly. If the egg was here, caution would have to govern his every move. No blunders, no mistakes. Maybe those who stole the egg were no more than bold and determined thieves, but maybe they were something more. He couldn't discount either possibility, not anymore.

But in any case, they came from a background and a land where intrigue was almost a way of life. They'd already proven their proficiency at that. Caution, he told himself again. He had to find a way to work from inside, a way to watch, give himself time. He turned off further thoughts as a crew of roustabouts began to tighten ring ropes, adjust tent poles, and hammer down stakes to prepare for the night's performance. A young woman set up a tall wooden box outside the entrance to the main tent, placed a roll of tickets atop the box, and herself on a tall stool. Fargo sauntered over to see a pretty enough face with too much makeup on it, dark round eyes, full cheeks, and short black hair. Lips that were very full gave her a perpetual half-pout, and a tight green dress clung to full breasts and a curvy, full-hipped figure.

"One, please," he said. "What time's the show?"

"Seven o'clock, an hour from now," she said, and her eyes moved up and down his tall frame with frank appreciation. "Be on time. It gets crowded," she told him.

"Then business must be good," Fargo commented.

"Yep. Word's gotten out. They're coming in from the outlying farms, too," she said, and her dark eyes studied him. She had a simple, unvarnished earthiness to her, he decided. "You're not from around here," she said.

"How do you know?" Fargo smiled.

"You're different. In my job, you get to tab the local types pretty quickly. Of course, they change with every town," she said. "I'm Frannie."

"Hello, Frannie. Fargo . . . Skye Fargo. Been with the circus long?"

"A good spell," Frannie said.

"I guess most of the acts have been with the circus for some time," he ventured, choosing words carefully.

"They come and go, some to different circuses, and new ones come to us," Frannie said.

"Which is your newest one, just out of curiosity?" Fargo asked blandly.

"Tanya, the high-wire aerialist," Frannie said.

Fargo kept his voice casual. "How long has she been with you?" he questioned.

"About six months," Frannie said. "She and Leonid."

"Who's Leonid?" Fargo frowned.

"Her uncle. He takes care of all her equipment, checks on the tightness of the trapezes, puts resin on the tightropes—all that kind of thing," Frannie said.

"Guess I'll see you later. I want to find a place to leave my horse," Fargo said.

"Real nice looking horse. There's an area back of the tent with a hitching bar," Frannie said, casting a sidelong glance at him. "What're you doing after the show?" she asked.

"Getting some sleep, I guess. Been riding long," he said.

"Mr. Kelly doesn't like us to go out with the customers. He wants us to stick to circus people, says it's better for us that way, but I could make an exception," Frannie said.

"Let's wait till after the show," Fargo replied as he led the Ovaro away. Frannie would be interesting, he was certain. She was without pretense. She didn't hide what she liked and he was sure she didn't hide what she disliked. But he didn't want any distractions, not yet, he told himself as he went behind the main tent and tethered the Ovaro to the long hitching bar. He idled, wasted time, and it was a little before seven when he returned to the main entrance of the tent to receive a wide smile from Frannie.

He found a seat at the end of one of the long wooden benches near the ring and watched the tent quickly fill up with the audience, including plenty of kids, he noted. Promptly at seven, four clowns came into the ring, each made up with a painted face and bulbous nose and each in a clown costume. They worked the audience for a while, mostly the kids, until finally a man ran into center ring dressed in a white spangled evening suit with a huge black bow tie and wearing a top hat.

"Welcome to Kelly's Circus, ladeeez and gents and all you youngsters. I'm Jim Kelly, and you've an evening of thrills and fun ahead of you." He was a man of some fifty years with gray hair visible when he removed his top hat, but he had a lean, spry figure and the youthful, debonair way of a master of ceremonies. Fargo sat back and found himself enjoying the circus as thoroughly as any of the youngsters in the audience.

Rudy the animal tamer and his tigers were on first. Tall, blond, and well-built, he faced the six tigers as they bounded from the wagons brought into the ring. Rudy was good, Fargo noted, the tigers viciously dangerous, and Fargo led the applause as the big cats were finally herded back into their cages. The four clowns kept the audience laughing between the acts. Finally the last act came and Fargo leaned forward in his seat.

"Tanya from Moscow in her death-defying aerial feats," Jim Kelly boomed, and the small figure that entered the ring in a deep red leotard seemed almost a child. Tanya was not more than five feet two inches tall, Fargo guessed, dark brown hair cut short, a thin nose, brown eyes, a clean-lined, pertly attractive face with a warm smile. As she effortlessly climbed a rope up to where the trapeze bars hung, he saw a lithe, trim body, beautifully proportioned and beautifully muscled, lovely long legs and breasts that, while smallish, were perfect for her taut body. There was something jewellike in her physical symmetry, he observed, and he took a moment to watch the short, square man with a lined face and long black hair who moved around the ring underneath Tanya, testing the tension on her equipment ropes. That would be the uncle, Leonid, Fargo guessed.

Tanya had reached the first trapeze and immediately went into her routines. She was more than good, he quickly saw. She was an excellent trapeze artist, flying with effortless ease from one trapeze to the next, executing faultless midair somersaults, twists, and turns. After the trapeze, she did a high-wire walking routine with grace and ease, making its perilousness seem inconsequential. Leonid, Fargo noted, watched her every move with intense concentration, his eyes going from the small, slender shape to flash to the various ropes and wires to check on their tension.

She drew a tremendous ovation when she finished, then slid down a long, angled wire to take her bows on the sawdust-covered floor of the ring. Again, Fargo was struck with the jewellike loveliness of her. The show ended with a fanfare from the two trumpets in the six-man band. He rose, a smile edging his lips. For a small traveling circus, it had been an entertaining show, right down to the young sandy-haired man who had performed an in-between-acts juggling routine. As he'd watched,

Fargo decided how to perhaps become an insider and get the time he needed to know Tanya. The one single question remained. . . . Was the lovely Tanya the end of the line for the priceless jeweled egg? Had she been chosen to keep it safe until a sale was arranged? Or was she but one more stop on the line? Was the egg here with her, or had she already passed it on to someone else?

Pavlev could have answered that, but he was history now. Tanya was the key for now, and as Fargo passed Frannie at the entranceway to the tent, she came forward to meet him. "Not tonight," he said with a smile. "But I'll be back in the morning. I might make it easier for you." Frannie frowned back, not understanding. "You said Mr. Kelly likes you to stick to circus people. I might be one of you by tomorrow," Fargo explained and hurried away. He took the Ovaro into the low hills, found a spot to bed down, and quickly sought sleep. He was up with the dawn and found a cleared circle of land where he began to ride the Ovaro as he hadn't ridden since he was a youngster—trick riding, hanging from the sides, doing saddle-vaulting and somersaults, suspending himself from the horse's powerful neck at a full gallop.

He stopped to rest himself and the horse after an hour, surprised and pleased with how well he had performed and how quickly it all came back. After he had rested, he put a half-dozen thin lengths of branch into the ground so that they stood some four feet high. He climbed back into the saddle then and sent the horse into a gallop around the six lengths of branch, firing as he rode and watching the branches disintegrate. Holstering the Colt, he reined to a halt and walked the horse to town. It was noon when he drew up before Jim Kelly, who was today considerably less resplendent in a tan shirt with suspenders attached to baggy trousers. The circus owner looked up and his eyes moved across the Ovaro's gleaming black fore- and hindquarters and pure white midsection.

"Mighty fine looking horse," he commented.

"He is that. Fit for a circus," Fargo said, and Jim Kelly's eyes questioned. "Name's Fargo . . . Skye Fargo. I saw the show last night, enjoyed it a lot. But there's something missing. You haven't a trick riding and fancy shooting act."

"And you and that handsome Ovaro can give me one," the circus master said.

"Bulls-eye," Fargo answered.

"All right, let's see what you can do," Jim Kelly said and strode into the main tent. Fargo followed and saw the sandy-haired young man watching with his juggling clubs in hand. Fargo paused in front of him.

"You want to help me out, young feller?" Fargo asked.

"Why not?" the young man responded. "How?"

"You've extra clubs?" Fargo questioned.

"A trunkful of them," the juggler answered.

"Good. I'll pay you for every one I use," Fargo said.

The young man's eyes broadened. "You a juggler too?" he asked.

"Not your kind of juggler," Fargo laughed. "Now, when I give you the signal, you go to the center of the ring and start juggling."

"Got it," the young man said, and as Fargo moved into the ring on the pinto he saw other figures gathering to watch. Frannie was one, along with two of the clowns in their oversize pants, a half-dozen roustabouts, and Tanya, looking just as jewellike in a white blouse that clung to her and a dark green skirt. He moved to one side of the ring, snapped a command at the Ovaro, dug knees into the horse's ribs, and was racing around the ring in seconds. He put on a dazzling display of trick riding, side-to-side acrobatics, standing on one leg on the saddle, executing a somersault at full gallop. When he finally drew to a halt, he motioned to the young man, who took the center of the ring and began to juggle his clubs. Fargo sent the pinto into a gallop once more, but this time he drew his Colt and fired as he circled the ring and the juggler's clubs exploded in midair as they were being juggled.

A spontaneous round of applause from the onlookers rose as he reined to a halt, and Jim Kelly stepped forward.. "Damned impressive, Fargo," the man said. "I'll give you our usual offer with new acts—a month's tryout to see what the audiences think, room and board only for that month. Pay after that if you stay."

"Fair enough," Fargo agreed.

"There's an empty living area in wagon three," Kelly said and strode away.

Fargo turned to the young juggler. "Thanks. Would you do the same at the end of every performance? I'll pay you for the clubs," Fargo said.

"Sure. It was fun. But you better keep shooting that way or I've a short career," the young man said. "I'm Paul Smith, by the way."

"Don't worry. You'll have a long career, Paul," Fargo said and turned to see Tanya still there.

"Welcome," she said with a shy smile, her accent even on the single word a little heavier than Galina's. "You are very good."

"So are you. I watched last night," Fargo said, and her smile grew less shy. "I'm Skye Fargo," he said as he swung from the saddle.

"Skye Fargo," she echoed, turning the name on her lips. "It is different from the American names I have heard," she said, tilting her head to give him a speculative glance. "I think maybe you are different, too," she remarked.

"Maybe we can find out," he said.

She gave a tiny shrug. "Maybe. Uncle Leonid might even approve of you. He does not like the American men who come around the circus."

"I'll do my best," Fargo said. "Where did you learn your English?"

"We played with a circus in London for a few years," Tanya said.

"You miss Russia?" Fargo asked casually.

"I visited a few months ago," she said, and he tucked the answer in a corner of his mind. A visit to make plans for a robbery? he wondered.

"I've got to find wagon number three," he said.

"I'll show you," Tanya said, and he stepped beside her as she led the way past the main tent. Some might have called her petite, but the description didn't fit the taut firmness of her, he decided. Glancing to his left, he saw Frannie watching, no half pout on her full lips now—only a glower of displeasure, and he was honestly sorry. He made a mental note to take her aside. Jealous women were always trouble and he didn't want that. He'd find something to tell her, he thought, Tanya led him to wagon number three, a long, closed, red-and-yellow wagon with two small windows, one at each end. "Good luck tonight," she said, and he watched her leave, her tight body moving with smooth ease.

He watched her go to another small cluster of wagons and enter one. Turning away, he opened the door to wagon three and found two doors off a tiny entranceway. One was closed, the other open, and he entered a living area where he had to bend his head or hit the ceiling. He saw two worn chairs and a table, a chipped low dresser and a bed that was only a little more than a cot. A small sink with a porcelain pitcher atop it took up another wall. It was, he suspected, living quarters for newcomers. He stepped outside, unsaddled the Ovaro, and took his gear into the wagon.

He rested till an hour before showtime, when he gave the Ovaro a fast grooming with the sweat scraper and used the stable rubber for a final polishing. Jim Kelly stopped by as he finished. "We usually close with Tanya, but I'm putting you on after her. That way we won't disturb the rhythm we have now," the circus owner said and hurried away. Fargo saddled up and used a double rig to give the saddle extra support for the strain he put on it in the trick riding. He'd just finished when Tanya came by, Leonid beside her.

"Tanya tells me you have joined our circus family," the man said, and his stolid appearance was belied by shrewd blue eyes. "Welcome."

"Thanks," Fargo said and was about to add more when Tanya's voice cut in, unmistakable tightness in it.

"He's back," she said, and Fargo saw her eyes on a man standing by the main tent, a huge figure, some six-feet three and two hundred and fifty pounds, Fargo guessed. He wore black trousers and a long black leather vest and had shaved his head almost to baldness.

"I'll get Mr. Kelly," Leonid said.

"No. He told you he cannot keep him away unless something bad happens," Tanya said.

"What's this all about?" Fargo questioned.

"His name is Brazos and he follows the circus because of me," Tanya said. "Leonid tried to chase him away and he almost broke Leonid's arm."

"He knocked out two of the roustabouts Mr. Kelly sent after him," Leonid said.

"What's he done to you?" Fargo asked Tanya.

"Nothing, yet. It's what he says, what he promises," she answered.

"Such as?"

"He says I will be his, that it has to be. He says he will take me away. Meanwhile, he is watching me and he says I must be friendly to him. I am afraid. He is mad," Tanya said.

"It is bothering Tanya's concentration. That could kill her on the trapeze or the high-wire," Leonid said.

"That puts a different face on it," Fargo said to Tanya. "You pay attention to your act and let me deal with this Brazos."

"Would you? I would be so grateful," Tanya said, her eyes round. "But he is very dangerous. You must be careful."

"I'm always careful," Fargo said, and Tanya's smile was already tinged with gratitude as she went off with Leonid.

Fargo's eyes went to take in the man again, but there was only emptiness where he had been. Fargo moved away, leading the pinto around the outer edges of the tent. But Brazos might well be a gift, he pondered. He wanted a way to get close to Tanya. What better path than earning her gratitude? He reached the back side of the tent and saw Frannie coming toward him. She threw him an icy glance as she passed, and he called to her. "Can we talk?" he asked.

She glared back. "No need. I was wrong about you. You only go for headliners, glamorous foreign types. Next time don't bother to act like you're interested."

He winced as he heard the hurt in her voice. "I wasn't acting," he said.

"Prove it. Meet me after the show," Frannie tossed back.

"I can't, not tonight," Fargo said. Frannie's pout turned icy and she stalked away. "Look, things aren't always what they seem," he called after her, knowing it was a weak offering.

"Go to hell," she flung back, not turning as she stepped into the tent. He swore silently and promised himself another try at her. He'd hurt her, not intentionally, and she was obviously easily hurt. That still left a jealous woman and a potential for trouble and he wanted to avoid that. The blare of trumpets broke into his thoughts. The show had begun. He led the Ovaro into the tent through a rear flap and settled down to wait where he could see the ring.

Everything went well, even though Rudy had a hard time with one of his tigers. Fargo felt himself enjoying the applause that followed his own act. Paul modestly shared his bow, holding the shattered juggling clubs aloft. When the crowd had left the tent and the roustabouts and cleaning men were doing their chores, Fargo unsaddled the Ovaro and tethered the horse on a long line outside his wagon. Inside, he unstrapped his gunbelt, took off his shirt, then realized he had to fill the big porcelain pitcher with water. He stepped from the wagon with it, started toward the water wagon he had noticed a few dozen yards away, and saw the small form in a short white nightgown that seemed even smaller beside the huge figure in the long black vest.

"Go away," Fargo heard Tanya say as he strode toward the water wagon.

"You don't want that," Brazos said. "You are just saying that."

"I think you ought to listen to the little lady," Fargo said and saw Brazos turn to him in surprise. The man had a heavy face, Fargo saw, with thick jowls, thick lips, and a broad nose under the close-cropped hair. Small eyes seemed even smaller in the thick face and they glittered with a strange wildness.

"Get out of here, whoever you are," Brazos growled.

"He is a friend of mine," Tanya put in and stepped toward Fargo.

The huge man took a step toward Fargo. "I will break you in half if you stay here," he said, and his big hands opened and clenched.

"Start breaking," Fargo said and let the pitcher slide to the ground. Brazos paused for a dozen seconds, his eyes growing smaller. He leaped forward with a sudden motion, raising both arms to stretch out his hands. Fargo stepped backwards, once, another step following the first, seeming suddenly afraid. Brazos' thick lips pulled back in a harsh grin and he rushed forward recklessly. He didn't see the short right uppercut that Fargo lifted almost from his knees, but he felt it crash into his jaw. He halted, quivered in place, and Fargo's left hook smashed into the side of his jaw.

Brazos half-turned as he stumbled backwards. Fargo knew the two blows would have put down most men but Brazos managed not to fall. Fargo stepped in, too quickly, and ran into a huge, treelike arm that swept around in a backward blow. He felt himself staggering back, off-balance, and tried to bring up another left hook as the huge man barreled at him. The blow skidded off the side of the man's face and the huge form slammed into him with the force of a charging buffalo. Fargo flew backwards, landed on his back, and just managed to get his left leg up as Brazos tried to fling himself over him. Fargo kicked out and caught Brazos in the stomach. Brazos let out a grunt of pain and missed landing fully atop his foe as Fargo rolled away. Fargo rolled again and jumped to his feet to see, with some surprise, that Brazos had regained his feet almost as quickly.

The man came at him again, no wild charges this time, but a series of powerful punches, dangerous despite their wildness. Fargo ducked under two and away from two more. He stepped in low and delivered a hard left to the man's ribs, followed by a smashing right. Brazos grunted in pain for a moment but he replied with a hooking right. Fargo managed to block the blow but the force of it sent him backwards and he felt the pain shoot through his forearm. He ducked another blow, then stepped in again to send a straight left into Brazos' stomach. Again, the man grunted but absorbed the blow and dived forward. Fargo tried to twist away from the huge bulk as it came at him, but slipped on one foot and felt himself go down as Brazos crashed into him.

This time the man was on top of him, and Fargo felt one treelike arm wrap around his neck. Immobilized by the man's weight, Fargo felt the arm tighten around his throat. He tried to pull the arm from around his throat but gave up the effort. Brazos was locked onto him and squeezing. Reaching up with his left arm, Fargo tried to seize the man's hair, only to remember that there was only a shaved stubble across the almost bald head. He was quickly losing breath, he knew, his throat beginning to burn. He couldn't get his powerful legs up to push because Brazos held him in place with his weight. Digging his hand into the ground, Fargo scraped up a handful of dirt, flung it up and backwards into the man's face. Brazos cursed and the arm around Fargo's neck loosened for an instant. It was enough and Fargo pulled away, kicking backwards as he flung himself to one side. Brazos missed as he tried to grab for him again.

Fargo leaped to his feet and turned to face the huge form as Brazos pushed himself up. The man came forward and this time Fargo stopped him with a sharp left jab. The blow made Brazos' head snap back, but the man answered with wild, swinging punches. Fargo danced away from the blows, getting in another jab that infuriated Brazos. The man rushed forward again, swinging, and again Fargo danced away, using only the left jab to pepper his opponent's face. Roaring with fury, Brazos came in with furious swings again. Each time Fargo danced away, answering only with the jab. But he saw what he wanted to see in Brazos' face. The man's mouth was open now and he was breathing hard, gulping in deep draughts of air. After his next half-dozen furious swings he halted, breathing heavily. Fargo hit him with another jab, this one sharper and harder. He saw the skin tear open on the man's cheek.

Brazos roared as he swung again, but his blows were slower and wilder now, and he halted again after the last flurry, the sound of his breathing harsh and very noticeable. Fargo weaved and threw a left hook with all the force of his shoulder behind it. It smashed into the point of Brazos' jaw and the man staggered backwards. Fargo's straight right landed in exactly the same place. Brazos staggered back again, and this time his arms dropped almost below his waist. Fargo smashed another left and then a right, punches landing again on the man's jaw, and Fargo saw the small eyes suddenly glaze over. Brazos' arms dropped to his sides and he swayed. With a final powerful left, the huge form collapsed, sinking to the ground with strange slowness to lie in a motionless heap.

Fargo looked up as Tanya rushed to cling to him, and he saw two roustabouts, Leonid, and to one side Frannie, with an empty pail in hand. "*Spasibo, spasibo,*" Tanya said, and Leonid came up and clasped his hand with both of his.

"Is very good, very wonderful," Leonid said. "You are good man, Fargo."

Tanya's arms came up to slide around his neck, and he felt the firmness of her against him. "Come visit tomorrow night, after we finish," she said, and Fargo nodded. She left then, Leonid walking behind her, carrying a bucket of water, and the two roustabouts nodded to him as they walked on. A muttered groan came to him, and he turned to see Brazos pushing himself to his feet, where he still swayed, his jaw already swollen.

"You won't have her," the man said thickly, blood dripping from his lips.

"I ever see you here again, I'll finish you," Fargo said. "Count on it."

Brazos stopped swaying, his small eyes pinpoints of hate, but he turned and lumbered away, stumbling as he did, and disappeared into the darkness. Frannie came forward with her pail and went to the water wagon, where she paused to glance at Fargo. "You did a good thing," she said. "But that doesn't change what I think."

"I'm sorry for that," Fargo said.

"I'm sure Miss Glamorous will be thanking you," Frannie said as she filled her pail.

"You're sounding jealous," Fargo said.

"I guess I am," Frannie said, starting back with the full pail of water.

He took the pail from her and walked beside her. "There's no need to be. You're attractive, sexy, appealing. You don't need to be jealous of anybody," he said.

"Then how come your eyes are only for Tanya?" Frannie asked with her simple directness.

He let a sigh escape him as he chose words. "Maybe we can talk about it sometime, but not now," he said.

"You telling me you've got some problem?" she pressed, frowning as she studied him.

"Maybe, in a way," he said. "I'm just saying you don't need to be jealous of anybody."

Frannie thought over his answers for a moment and he halted before the wagon, where she stopped and took the pail from him. "I'm still jealous," she said. "But I'll think about it." She hurried into the wagon as Fargo walked away and let himself feel a moment of satisfaction. He'd calmed Frannie some . . . as much as possible for the moment. She'd be hurt but would keep it to herself, he felt confident. And he'd taken the first giant step to reach Tanya. He felt good as he returned to his wagon and slept. Maybe the end of the sawdust trail was at hand.

7

Word of his fight with Brazos had traveled quickly, and the next day he found himself congratulated by most everyone in the circus, starting with Jim Kelly. It also gave him a chance to meet with other members of the troupe: Pete, Pat, Harry, and Lou, the four clowns; Paolo, Carlos, and Vincent, the three acrobats from Venice; and many others, from members of the band to roustabouts. The feeling that there was a circus family came across very strongly, and his action with Brazos had given him a new acceptance.

He came upon Tanya doing her exercises, clad in a short yellow outfit that clung to her and left firm, lithe legs exposed. "Later tonight, remember," she murmured.

"I wouldn't be forgetting," he told her as he went on. Frannie, sitting beside the ticket box, glanced at him but her usual pout had replaced anger and he was pleased at that. He spent the afternoon currying the Ovaro and the horse glistened by showtime.

Again, with Paul Smith juggling at the close, Fargo heard the audience's applause and understood the rewards of the entertainer as he never had before. After he'd unsaddled and fed the pinto, he made his way to Tanya's wagon. She wore the rehearsal outfit that fit her as though it were another skin, and she let him in with a warm smile and her light brown eyes wide with welcome. Her quarters were decorated with colored pillows and bright blankets, a wide bed against one wall with the dresser alongside it. She took a bottle and two shot glasses from the top of the dresser, turning her back to him for a moment, and he admired the slenderness of her waist as it curved into a fittingly small yet very round rear.

"Vodka," Tanya said, turning to him. "You have had it?"

"What passes here," Fargo said. "Not the real thing."

"This is the real thing. This is a vodka we call *zubrowka*," she said, handing him one of the filled shot glasses. She sat down on the edge of the bed and motioned to him to sit beside her. She raised her glass in a toast as he did. "*Nazdarovya*," she said.

"Bottoms up," he returned and took a long draw of the vodka and felt the strength of it spread through him, matching any tequila he'd ever had.

She took another pull on her glass and her light brown eyes were wide and suddenly grave. "It was a wonderful thing you did for me last night, Fargo," she said, and suddenly she leaned forward and her lips were on his, a soft, brief moment, and then she pulled back. "It is the only way I can thank you and it is not enough," she said.

"It'll do fine," Fargo said and watched as she curled her legs under her and her smallish yet perfect breasts pushed against the fabric with a little-girl piquantness. She made him think of a perfectly modeled porcelain figurine. "Tell me about Tanya," he said. "I've never known an aerialist, much less a Russian one. You said you worked for a London circus. What made you come here?"

"I wanted a change and I always wanted to see America. Traveling with a circus is a good way to do this," Tanya said.

"It is," Fargo agreed. It was an answer he would have accepted as a simple truth if there had been no Pavlev and no sawdust trail. "You going to stay here with the circus?" he asked.

"I don't know," Tanya answered, taking another draw of her vodka. "This is very far from my homeland. From Europe, I could return to Moscow in a week. I might get homesick here."

Fargo smiled. It was a completely reasonable answer. But then Galina had always given him reasonable answers that weren't quite the truth. Perhaps reasonableness was a part of Russian intrigue, he reflected. "I hope you stay," he said. "You told me Leonid doesn't like the American men who come around. What about you?"

"I agreed with Leonid," Tanya said. "Until now." She smiled and there was an elfin mischievousness in her face that was definitely not little girl like.

"Let's go riding in the morning," Fargo suggested. "I'm sure the circus has extra horses you can borrow."

"I'd like that," Tanya said. "It'll be good to get away for a while." She finished her vodka, and he drained his glass as he watched her swing the lithe, lovely legs from under her to the floor. He stood up with her. She was so small and yet there was nothing of the helplessness about her that so often went with small girls. "Nine o'clock?" she asked, and he nodded. She reached up, brushed his lips with hers again. "Thank you again for everything," she said softly.

"Good night," he said.

"*Spokonoi notchi,*" she answered, and he strode from the wagon to his own. He undressed and stretched out and felt good. It was going well, but he had to be careful not to press too hard. Questions had to be formed so they wouldn't arouse suspicions, on her part or on Leonid's if she discussed them with him. Tanya had an open, wide-eyed innocence to her that made Fargo wonder if she were involved in more than she realized. Perhaps she was being used. The possibility was real enough and he went to sleep on the thought.

Morning came warm and bright, and Tanya met him sitting atop one of the circus horses that had the wide, thick body and heavy legs of mixed Percheron and saddle-horse blood. She wore a pale yellow shirt and dark brown riding britches, obviously of Russian design. She looked even smaller on the big horse, but she handled the animal with firm ease, Fargo noted as he led her from town and into the hills, where he found a spot in a stand of Engelmann spruce that let them look out over the majesty of the rolling hills made of quaking aspen, silver fir, hawthorn, and mountain ash.

"It is very beautiful, but what about Indians? I hear they are always a danger," Tanya said.

"The Indians around here aren't going to bother us," he told her. "They made their peace with the white man in this part of the country." She walked forward through the spruce, satisfied at his answer, seeming very much at peace, and looking very lovely in her porcelain-figurine way.

"It reminds me of walking through the forests outside Moscow and to the north. It is big and deep and makes you feel very small," Tanya said.

"You ever think about staying here?" Fargo queried. "Many people who come from overseas come to stay."

Her little smile was wistful. "No, I will go back to my homeland. It is too much inside me."

"When?" he inquired casually. "Soon?"

"Not so soon. A year, perhaps. Two, maybe. I don't know," she said, and Fargo's lips pursed. It was not an answer he'd expected. The thieves who stole the jeweled egg wouldn't wait two years to sell it, not even one year. Did that mean Tanya was not really involved? he wondered.

"What's going to make you decide when?" he slid at her.

"A time will come and I'll know, from outside or from inside," she said, and Fargo wondered if perhaps his attention should be turned to Leonid. She swept away his thoughts by taking his hand to climb up the steep hills. She thoroughly enjoyed the wildness, the beauty of lavender penstemons and orange Indian paintbrushes, the quiet loveliness of mountain streams filled with brook trout. Her hand stayed in his most of the time and the day went quickly. "Can we do this again tomorrow morning?" she asked when they returned to the circus grounds.

"Why not?" he said. "I'll find another place to explore."

She hurried off to her wagon and Fargo returned to his, where he gave the Ovaro a quick rubdown. The evening's show had a good crowd and went off perfectly. The day had set a pattern that was to follow during the rest of the week. He'd go riding with Tanya in the mornings and they'd return in time for the night's show. He was beginning to feel like a regular circus performer when Paul sent away for a new supply of juggler's clubs. Frannie continued to ignore him, but he saw that she was aware of his riding out with Tanya every morning. More importantly, he had established a warm relationship with Tanya, warm enough so that she ended each day with a quick kiss and warm enough so that he felt he could dig a little more without arousing suspicion.

"You ever see anyone from Russia?" he asked as they rode one day.

"Why do you ask that?" Tanya returned at once, and he was disappointed at the sharpness of her reaction.

"Just wondered," he answered calmly. "There are more than a few people from your country in this area. I've seen them myself, especially in Eugene. Most all the trading clippers from Russia dock at Depoe Bay. I just thought you might have met a few countrymen."

"Only a few," she said, but her voice had relaxed and he was grateful for that.

"Guess maybe I've met more than you have," Fargo said casually.

"I've kept close to the circus. We don't really meet many people outside ourselves," Tanya said. When they reached the circus grounds, her kiss was as warm as usual, and he breathed an inner sigh of relief at that. Later, alone, he grimaced as he thought about the sharpness of her original reaction. It had been instantaneous and its message was that Tanya was not as uninvolved as he'd come to hope. The feeling was reinforced a day later. "I cannot go riding tomorrow," she had told him, and he let his brows lift. "I have to wait for someone to pay a visit," she said.

"Sorry for that," Fargo smiled. "Maybe the day after."

"Yes, I'm sure that will be fine," Tanya said, and he went on his way.

The next day he rode out alone, but he didn't go far, turning up into the hills to halt at a spot that gave him a good view of the town and the circus tents. He saw nothing but the usual wagons and riders moving in and out of town, and he returned late that afternoon to see Tanya standing outside her wagon. Her brow wore a tiny wrinkle and he saw the tension in her body.

"Shouldn't you be changing into your costume?" he asked. "There's not much time left."

"Yes," she said, the wrinkle staying on her brow as her eyes continued to sweep the town streets within her view.

"Still waiting for somebody?" he remarked.

"Yes, but he's always here long before this. It is plain he is not coming," Tanya said.

"You're worried about that," Fargo ventured.

She gave a little shrug. "A little. He has always been on time."

Dead men seldom are, Fargo thought to himself. "It was important he come, it seems," Fargo remarked aloud.

Tanya gave another shrug, but a wariness came into her eyes. "He refinishes my high-wire shoes," she said.

Fargo nodded. "That is important," he said. She had given him a good answer without hesitation. Was it one that had been used to explain Pavlev's former visits? he wondered. Tanya turned and hurried into her wagon, and Fargo walked on with an unhappy grimness inside himself. He couldn't see Tanya as part of a gang of international thieves, not with her eager, open warmth. Yet she was connected, somehow, someway, he was becoming certain.

When morning came she was her usual happy, warm self, and she made no reference to the previous day's disappointment. She wasn't acting, putting on a false front, he was sure. There were two parts to her: the talented, happy circus performer here in America, a visitor from a foreign country; and another hidden part, and she managed to keep them separate enough. Only they weren't separate, and he'd have to reach into that other part. The final question still hung in the air. Was the egg here with her, or was she still but one more link in a chain? When the day ended with Tanya growing closer to him as she had each day, he decided he'd use the next few days to move more boldly with her. When her lips brushed his, he pulled her tighter, pressed harder, and saw the moment of surprise in her eyes.

But she didn't pull away, and when he stepped back he saw her eyes smoldering with new fires. When they rode south the next day to stop beside a pond, he held her again, and she answered with her lips opening for him. When she finally pulled back, she stretched out beside him at the edge of the pond, her eyes searching his. "I do not know what to do about myself," she said. "You make me want you, but I am not ready."

"If you want, you're ready, I'd say," Fargo answered.

She glanced away a moment. "It is not that simple," she said. The surge of excitement pulled at him. She was toying with confiding in him, yet was holding back. He had to be careful. He had to walk his own tightrope.

"What's not simple about it?" he asked, keeping his tone casual, almost amused.

Tanya's eyes found his, very round and wide, and she peered hard at him and blinked before answering. "I can't tell you, not now. Just believe me. There are things in the way."

"Not to me," he said, leaned over and found her lips with his. She didn't respond at first, then her lips parted and her arms went around his neck, firm strength in their touch, and she was letting him explore her mouth with his tongue. Finally she pulled away, small breasts under the shirt rising and falling as she drew in deep gasps of breath. "I'd say not to you, either," he murmured.

She sat up. "Perhaps not. But I need a little more time to think, Fargo. Please . . ."

Her voice and her face were suddenly those of a little girl unsure of the world and of herself. He'd ease off, but only for the moment, he decided. He rode back to the circus with her, feeling slightly smug and slightly shoddy. But then, it was not the first time he'd felt shoddy carrying through a job he'd promised to do. . . .

It was only a night later when the unexpected surfaced, first in the person of Frannie, a few minutes before showtime. "I have to talk to you. It concerns Tanya," she said, her dark eyes round under a wrinkled brow.

"The time's not right, Frannie. Not yet, not now," he told her.

"Yes, now. Brazos is back. He's here," Frannie said.

The frown dug into Fargo's brow. "You sure?" he asked in astonishment.

"I'm sure. I told Mr. Kelly and he went looking for him, but he didn't find him. He said I was imagining things."

"But you weren't."

"No, dammit. I saw him. He's back and I don't think it's to see the circus," Frannie snapped.

Fargo's mouth became a thin line. Frannie wasn't the kind to imagine things. "All right, get back and take tickets. I'll find him," Fargo said and headed for the back section of the main tent, where everyone gathered to wait before going on. He reached the area, peered past the acrobats and Ahmed the sword-swallower, and found Tanya, doing knee bends as she waited. He scanned the dark shadows around the tent and saw no lurking figure, left the Ovaro with its reins curled around a tent pole, and hurried away on foot. Tanya's wagon his next stop, he came up pressed along the side until he reached the lone window, where he had to rise up on his toes to peer in.

Her quarters inside were empty, and he turned from the window to move forward again, still pressed against the outside of the wagon. One hand resting on the butt of the Colt, he turned the corner of the wagon, but again there was no one waiting there. He heard the band playing the music for the acrobats as he went around to the rear of the wagon, and again no one waited there.

He began to move forward in a systematic search of the other circus wagons: the haulage drays, the barred animal wagons with their pacing tigers, the circus owner's colorful rig, the high-sided wagon that held the band. He peered inside each, circled each, scanned the dark shadows that reached out from each, and only went on to the next when he was satisfied no one hid in waiting. He listened to the circus band playing in the background, the music for Ahmed, then that for the parade of elephants. Tanya would be going on next, and his lips pulled back in a grimace.

Perhaps Brazos was watching from the audience, he speculated. He had only two more wagons to check out. He ran to the first and found nothing. The second was the long, brightly painted wagon that served as living quarters for the four clowns. It had four doors, one for each living space, and he yanked open the first, then the second and third, and then the fourth. He had slammed the fourth door closed and started to turn away when he spun around and pulled the door open again. A pair of shoes had poked out from beneath the bed, but they weren't the oversize, floppy clown's shoes. They were ordinary walking shoes. Crossing the small space in two long-legged strides, Fargo leaned down and pulled the shoes out from under the bed—only to find a pair of ankles came with them. He swore softly and pulled again and legs and a body followed. Fargo stared down at the man and recognized him at once.

It was Harry, one of the four clowns, and a line of red ran down the side of his face where he had been struck on the temple. He was still dressed in his street clothes, Fargo saw, and unconscious but still alive. Cursing, Fargo spun and ran from the wagon. There was no time to tend to the clown as ominous misgivings pulled at him.

Harry's clown costume was the biggest and baggiest of all the clown outfits, bright yellow with red polka dots, and he sported a bulbous red nose and a wig of unruly curly hair, along with his usual clown facial makeup. As he ran towards the main tent, he heard Tanya's music from the band. She had just begun her act. He raced into the tent, then came to a halt, his eyes sweeping the audience where the clowns usually worked and mingled. He spotted Pat in his white-and-blue outfit with peaked dunce cap, then Lou in his black-and-white harlequin costume and clown face makeup. His eyes swept the audience again and he spotted Pete on the other side of the tent, four rows up in the benches.

Bringing his eyes down, he scanned the ring again and suddenly the flash of yellow was there before him, some twenty yards away. Brazos was on the floor of the tent, kneeling beside one of the wooden pegs driven into the ground all around the ring. Fargo's gaze went to the rope tied to the peg, followed it upwards, and saw it was one of the ropes holding the high-wire taut and in place. He snapped his eyes back to Brazos and saw the movement of the man's right arm inside the billowy yellow costume, short back-and-forth motions. Fargo cursed through lips that were pulled back. Brazos was cutting the rope that ran to the high-wire.

His words blazed inside Fargo. *You won't have her.* Cursing, Fargo drew the Colt as his eyes flicked upwards to the high-wire. Tanya was balancing herself, halfway through her death-defying journey, and Fargo returned his eyes to Brazos—but his finger trembled against the trigger. A shot would do more than startle Tanya. It would shatter her absolute concentration, destroy her delicate balance, and send her plunging from the wire in a fatal misstep. He dropped the Colt back into its holster and yanked the throwing knife from its strap around his calf. Racing forward around the edge of the ring, he cast another glance at Tanya. She had paused on the wire, adjusting her balance, and Fargo raced on, the faces of the audience becoming a blur.

Brazos continued to work at severing the rope, Fargo saw, and he was but a half-dozen yards from the man when Brazos turned and saw him, somehow suddenly sensing danger. Even with his bulbous clown's nose that covered half his face and the clown makeup, Fargo saw his small eyes glittering insanely. Fargo flung a curse at the man as he flung the thin, double-edged blade through the air with all the strength of his arm and shoulder behind it. Brazos saw the blade coming at him and began to drop down, but the knife cut through the air as though it were a bullet. It smashed into Brazos' face as he tried to duck below it, cut the bulbous clown's nose in two, and imbedded itself to the hilt, the point stabbing into the top of his trachea.

His mouth dropped open and he made hoarse, choking noises as he collapsed, but Fargo's eyes were on the nearly severed rope. The last strands, almost cut through, were shredding by themselves now, unraveling with the tension on them. With a roar of despair, Fargo hurled himself forward in a flying dive. He hit the ground on his stomach alongside the peg, sending a spray of sawdust into the air, reached out and got one hand around the rope, then the other, just as the last strand unraveled from the peg. He lay half on his stomach, half on his side, pulling on the rope with all his strength, arms stretched out until it seemed they'd tear loose from his shoulder sockets. He glimpsed Tanya at the ceiling of the tent, saw her waver for an instant as the tension of the guy rope changed. Then with three quick steps she reached the platform by the center pole, just as the roustabouts and Leonid raced up to take hold of the rope.

Four of them held it tight as a fifth pounded another peg into the ground. Fargo released his hold. His arms fell to his sides and he felt the trembling in them of muscles strained to the tearing point. He lay for a moment and watched the others secure the rope to the new peg and then pushed himself to his feet. He saw Tanya sliding to the ground on the descent wire and he turned to Brazos, the bulbous clown nose cut in half and a line of red pouring from his open mouth, the knife handle sticking upwards. Little round splashes of red were mingling with the red dots on the baggy yellow costume. He had masqueraded as a clown, a figure of laughter and warmth, to kill. It seemed fitting that death should bestow the final mockery.

Fargo turned away as Tanya flew into his arms. The circus band played louder and faster as he walked away with her and the others carried Brazos off in a sheet. Jim Kelly stepped in front of him as he neared the rear of the tent. "That was something special, real special," the circus owner said. "I'll cancel your act tonight."

"No," Fargo heard himself saying, surprised at his own words. "Hell, I'm a circus performer. The show must go on." He shook his arms vigorously as he left Tanya and strode to the Ovaro. A new surge of strength pounding through him, he sent the Ovaro prancing to the center of the ring and went into his routine. He cut down only a little, not enough for anyone to be disappointed, and received the usual round of cheers when he finished. He rode from the ring and dismounted to find Tanya waiting.

"Come to my wagon tonight," she said.

"Feel like a little celebrating?" he asked.

"A lot of celebrating," she said, and her eyes were both grave and dancing.

"I'll be along," he told her and led the Ovaro from the tent. His gaze swept the crowds as they departed and found Frannie's curvy, fulsome figure counting ticket stubs. She glanced up as he stopped beside her.

"You were something. She owes you her life," Frannie said. "I hope she realizes it."

"No, she owes *you* her life, and I'll see that she knows that," Fargo said. "If you hadn't told me, Brazos would have had it all his way. You'd told Kelly. You could've left it at that, especially feeling the way you do. But you didn't and that was a class thing."

Frannie gave a slight shrug. "I have to look in the mirror every morning," she said. He reached forward and kissed her gently. "What was that for?" she asked, and he heard the hope under the flippancy.

"For being you. For doing the right thing," he said.

"But you're still after her," Frannie said, the pout returning.

"There are still reasons. I'll tell you about them someday. Promise," he said. She returned to counting tickets, dismissal in her manner, and he hurried away.

8

Tanya opened the door at his knock and he stepped into the wagon, where a lamp burned on low. She stood before him, barefoot, wearing a thin pink nightgown that rested lightly on the pointy tips of her small breasts. Her eyes searched his face for a moment and then her arms lifted, encircling his neck as she rose on tiptoes and pressed her mouth to his. He felt her lips move, open, felt the touch of her tongue for an instant. "What happened to more time to think?" he remarked.

"Gone," Tanya said, and her arms lowered and she began to unbutton his shirt. She pulled the garment from him and her eyes admired the smooth, muscled contours of his chest. Her hands moved across his pectorals, pressing, a strong yet sensitive touch. He let his gunbelt drop to the ground, followed by his trousers, and as he kicked off his boots, she lifted the pink nightgown and tossed it aside.

He feasted his eyes on her diminutive loveliness; her lithe, slender figure was perfectly sculpted, her skin a soft white and absolutely unblemished. Naked, the smallish breasts were no longer small but perfect for her, standing out with pointed firmness, nipples small and pale pink on even paler pink areolas. Her waist was slender, ribs showing slightly, abdomen flat, legs slender, muscled yet beautifully curved, and in between narrow hips was a surprisingly luxuriant V-shaped patch. She could have been a little figurine carved out of white ivory by a master artist, except for the fact that she beckoned with living, simmering want, her eyes boring into him with pinpoints of desire. He reached out, touched her shoulders, and she was warm as he pulled her to him and fell backwards onto the bed with her. He wondered if he'd have to be careful with her jewellike delicacy, but she quickly flung the thought from him as her mouth pressed hard against his and strong arms circled him.

"*Da, da . . .*" Tanya breathed as her lips opened, her tongue darting out almost frantically, and he felt the strength in her small body as her hands rubbed up and down his torso. When his mouth left hers to find one petite breast, she threw her head back and a half laugh, half scream of delight came from her. "*Yestcho . . . yestcho . . .* more," she cried out as he took the pointed breast deep into his mouth, caressed the tiny nipple with his tongue and felt it harden. "Yes, yes . . . *da,*" she murmured, and he felt the firmness of her as he ran his hands down her body, tight muscles beneath the soft, pale white skin. His mouth continued to caress her breasts as his hand found the small but luxuriant patch and pressed through it, rested on the firm rise of her venus mound, edged further downwards and felt the moistness of her.

"Oh, oh, yes . . . *da, da, da . . . khorosho, khorosho . . .* " Tanya suddenly half-screamed and her hips rose, twisted, her legs coming up, falling open and slamming together, opening again and slamming shut again. Her entire body began to writhe and twist and her hands were moving up and down his skin, clutching, pressing, palms digging hard into him. Suddenly she reached down, found him, curled her hand around his vibrant throbbing, and she gave a cry of pure delight. She all but tore from his arms, swung her lithe little body around and was atop him, guiding him into her with a yell of triumph. She was all but leaping as she plunged herself down onto him. "Aaaaahhh . . . " she cried out as he filled her and felt her sweet warm walls against him, rubbing, sliding, flesh caressing flesh, senses inflaming senses. Her legs were drawn up, as if she were riding a stallion, and he felt her small yet very round rear slam down onto his legs as she bucked and tossed and bucked again, and she was gasping out tiny sounds, her brown hair bouncing in all directions.

Suddenly she pulled her torso away from him, leaned herself backwards along his legs while keeping her tight warmth around him, and began to slide back and forth, creating still another wonderful sensory touching, until finally she pushed herself upwards again and brought the small pointed breasts down to his lips once more. His hands closed around her round rear and stayed there as it rose and fell. Suddenly he felt a new trembling in her body, a series of inner contractions that matched the outer tremors. He pushed himself up, turned her onto her back, and plunged deeper, drew back and plunged again and again, and Tanya's small body leaped and bucked with him, her legs lifted to encircle the small of his back. "Good . . . good . . . good," she breathed, tiny gasped words, and her arms kept his face against her breasts. Suddenly he felt her pubic mound lift and a spiraling cry rose from her. He felt the sweet contractions of her and then she slid herself backwards as her entire body trembled and she held herself poised, almost outside of him, the vibrating head resting against the deliciously soft lips.

She stayed poised, held herself there, on the very edge

of absolute ecstasy, as if she were on the high-wire, balanced on the edge of life and death, and then, with a scream of total ecstasy, every sense in her jewellike body released, she plunged forward and he met her with his own explosion. "Yes, *da, da,* yes . . . oh, God, good, oh . . . aiiiie," Tanya gasped out as she clung to him, trembling violently, the small, pointed breasts quivering, and the blinding, all-encompassing moment locked them together, that singular embrace unlike any other. Finally, with a small, reluctant sigh, Tanya's arms and legs fell away from him and she stretched out, her eyes finding his as a tiny smile played across her face. "You are surprised," she said.

"I guess you could say that," Fargo admitted. "But it sure was a pleasant one."

"For me, too," she said as he settled down beside her and admired the exquisite loveliness of her body, deciding she had to be as beautifully perfect as any of the jewels in the precious egg he sought. "I won't be happy with only this night," she said.

"I was thinking the same thing," he said, and she curled against him, pale pink nipples touching his chest. "Maybe I can stop you from being homesick," he said, and she gave a shrug with her little laugh.

"I don't know, but I know I want you to keep trying," she said.

"Tell me about life in Russia," Fargo explored. "I met a man from Russia some years ago. He said Russia was a fine place to live and the czar was a just and honorable man."

Tanya pulled away from him and sat up, her pointed breasts hardly swaying as she frowned at him. "He wasn't Russian," she said.

"Oh, he was Russian, all right," Fargo said.

"Then he must have been one of the czar's distant relatives. There are a lot of those," Tanya said.

"You saying the czar isn't a just and honorable man?" Fargo pressed.

"He is a tyrant, a despot. Only the rich are happy in Russia. The peasants and the poor people are at the mercy of the czar and his generals and tax collectors. You cannot imagine what it is like. It is a different world here in America."

"Tell me what it's like," Fargo said.

"The little people have no rights at all. The czar's cossacks are the worst of all. They sweep through a village whenever they feel like it, demanding money, gold, food. They take whatever women they want, enjoy them and throw them back. Sometimes they kill them. Then they ride on."

"Did they take you?" Fargo asked.

Tanya's eyes had grown dark with hate, he saw, and her hands were clenched into little fists. "Almost. They swept through my village one night, but I got away. My sister wasn't so lucky. Her husband tried to stop them and they killed him."

"Anyone ever try going to the czar with these stories?" Fargo queried. "Maybe he doesn't know what goes on."

Tanya's little laugh was harsh. "He doesn't want to know. It is easier for him this way. His cossacks and his generals can do what they want and they stay happy and loyal."

"Maybe if a whole village stood up to him and complained he'd listen," Fargo suggested.

"That's been tried and the leaders were always singled out and shot," Tanya said. "Because in every village or in every region, the czar has someone in his pay who reports to him or the local general. It becomes hard to trust anyone, and so the people do nothing out of fear for their lives and the lives of their families."

Fargo paused, marshaling thoughts and words. "It sounds like a lot of people would like to strike back at the czar," he said.

Tanya's eyes suddenly grew wary. "What do you mean by strike back?" she asked.

"Do something to make him unhappy," Fargo said airily. "Steal the crown jewels, kidnap the czarina, whatever."

Tanya's eyes softened and a smile came to her lips. "I think he would be more upset at losing the crown jewels than the czarina." she said. "But there's little chance of either happening." She reached over, picked up his shirt and handed it to him. "I wish you could stay but I wouldn't want you seen leaving my wagon in the morning. We don't want to start tongues wagging yet."

"Guess not," he said and began to dress. "By the way, you ought to thank Frannie. She's the one who told me Brazos had come back."

"I'm surprised. She's never liked me. She's never tried to be friendly," Tanya said.

"Frannie's got a wide jealous streak, but when the chips were down she came through," Fargo said as he strapped on his gunbelt.

"I'll visit her tomorrow," Tanya said and walked to the door with him, looking deliciously lovely in her naked perfection. "Tomorrow night?"

"Count on it," he said as he stepped from the wagon. He crossed the circus grounds, now dark and silent except for a low growl from the tigers' cages. Once inside his wagon, he undressed again and stretched out on the bed. Tanya's lovely body and her acrobatic passion sweeping back over him. But her description of her homeland also returned. She had painted a very different picture of the czar than Galina had. Her intensity made him feel that Tanya's picture was closer to the real one. But it had also made him certain she was involved in the theft, perhaps in a peripheral way, but involved, and he thought of how wary her eyes had become when he mentioned striking back at the czar. He had hit close to home.

But she cared for him now. Trust had been created. If the egg were here, he'd have it soon, he was certain, and he would have been right about getting back at the czar. He had to discount the strange things Pavlev and the others had said and done. It was shaping up as a plain high-stakes robbery, as Galina had said it was. Perhaps the thieves had taken a personal satisfaction beyond the money to be made, but that didn't change the face of it. He could only hope now that Tanya's involvement was that of a minor player. Besides, bringing the egg back to Galina and Nicholas would end it, he felt certain. They'd be happy to make tracks for Russia with their precious jeweled trophy. He slept confident he was close to getting the egg and hopeful that Tanya was essentially an outsider. He had come to feel a sympathy for her. Even with all her performing talents and her petite exquisiteness, she seemed a lost soul trying to refind roots.

In the morning he tended to grooming the Ovaro and only glimpsed Tanya from a distance, Leonid dogging her steps, and he wondered if the man had seen him leaving her wagon. Leonid didn't like outsiders, Tanya had told him, and now he knew the man's real reasons. Thieves were always distrustful and Leonid was part of it, even if only a small part. Perhaps his job was to watch over Tanya. Fargo pushed aside further wonderings and didn't see Tanya again until it was time for her to perform. She did her usual wonderful job, with an added set of trapeze maneuvers that held everyone spellbound. He went on after her and when the show was over wandered to her tent. Tanya opened at his knock, but she wore no pink nightgown tonight. Instead, she had on the yellow blouse and dark brown skirt, and he noticed her eyes searching his face as he stepped into the wagon.

He reached for her and she came to him with a stiffness. He halted before his lips found hers. "We have to talk first," she said, and he stepped back.

"Leonid been giving you a hard time?" Fargo questioned.

"No, it has nothing to do with Leonid. I went to see Frannie but I never did talk to her," Tanya said, and Fargo cocked an eyebrow. "She was talking to Mr. Kelly. I stopped and I couldn't help hearing them. He apologized for not having believed her and thanked her for going to you about Brazos."

"Nothing wrong in that," Fargo said.

"She told him she and you were very close. She said you had told her you had your own reasons for seeing me," Tanya said, and Fargo silently cursed. *Damn you, Frannie. Damn your need to polish your image. Damn your jealousy.* "What are those reasons, Fargo? What did you mean by that?" Tanya pressed.

"She misunderstood what I told her," Fargo said.

Tanya's eyes continued to search his face. "Last night you asked so many questions about Russia, about how it was there, how I felt about my homeland and about the czar. I wondered about it later, but I was glad. I liked your asking. Now I wonder about it again, but I am not glad."

"Just questions, that's all," Fargo said and cursed silently again as Tanya continued to study him.

"No, not just questions, I'm afraid. I have been thinking back, about how you suddenly appeared. It was not needing a job that brought you here to the circus, was it?" she challenged, and he realized he couldn't find the words for a convincing denial and Tanya was too astute for glibness. The time had come, he decided, to use the truth to pin her down.

"No, it wasn't," he admitted.

"The truth is, you've never been in a circus before, have you?" Tanya pressed.

"Right again," he said. "I came to find you."

"Why?"

"I was hired to get the egg back," Fargo said.

She let her eyebrows lift. "Egg? What egg?" she asked.

He let a sigh of patient tolerance escape him. "The trail led here," he said. "Pavlev is dead. Most of the others, too." He peered hard at her, tried to spot a flinch, a moment of dismay registering in her face. But there was none. She held to her mask.

"This means nothing to me," she said.

"No more lies, Tanya. It's too late. Just give me the egg," Fargo said.

She shrugged. "You have made some kind of terrible mistake," she said. "You say you were hired? Who hired you?"

"You know who hired me, Tanya. The czar's people, here to get the egg," Fargo said.

"I don't know anything about this. You see, you didn't have to sleep with me for this," she answered with an edge of hurt in her voice.

"I didn't sleep with you for this," he answered and knew it was only a half-truth.

"You've made a mistake. Please leave, Fargo. I must wonder now if you only saved my life to get this imaginary egg you talk about," she said reproachfully.

"You don't believe that," he said and saw the pain in her eyes.

"I don't know what to believe, but I know you were not honest with me," she said, and he searched for other words to reach her.

"There's no place left to run, Tanya. I'll see that you're kept out of it. Give me the egg and it'll be over. There'll be no more danger to you," he said.

She frowned and he saw disdain in her eyes. "Can you think Tanya is afraid of danger?" she threw back at him, and his lips tightened, visions of her flying through the air flashing in his mind.

"No, I guess that was a pretty dumb thing to say," he admitted. "But is it worth going on? Will you get that much money out of it?"

"How American. You think everything is done for money," she snapped.

"Stealing usually is," he returned and again saw the disdain in her eyes. Her words hung inside him, a kind of echo of the attitude Pavlev and the others had. Danger, sacrificing one's life, they seemed almost expected. Again, that was not the way of most thieves. She opened the door and held it open, and a sadness came into her face.

"You saved my life. I will always be grateful to you for that. I cannot be grateful for anything else. Please go," she said.

He walked from the wagon and paused to glance back. "I'll be back. I'll make you listen to me, for your sake," he said. She closed the door and he walked into the darkness.

She had denied knowing about the egg, accused him of being entirely mistaken, and she'd held to the mask she had put on. But she was lying, he was certain. She lied with the same implacable dedication Pavlev and Dmitri had shown with their lives. "Damn," he bit out. He had concluded it had been a theft for money, a carefully planned and well-executed piece of thievery. But now, once again, he found himself with inner wonderings and knew he had to do two things: one, get to Tanya again, and two, keep a closer watch on her. He couldn't do less now, though he still wanted to help her, and when he returned to his wagon he took his bedroll and went out into the night with it. He set it down in a thicket of shadbush from which he could see Tanya's wagon below.

He settled down and kept watch until the sun came up, then returned to his wagon and stole a few hours of sleep. When he awoke and had quickly washed and dressed, he went outside and his eyes swept the circus grounds. Rudy was feeding his big cats, the Risselli brothers were practicing new routines, Ahmad was polishing his swords, and everyone was busy at their own chores. He found Tanya exercising near her wagon, Leonid standing by. Fargo started to walk toward her but she glanced up, saw him, and went into the wagon, the gesture unmistakably rejection. He turned away and decided to wait till after the show.

Taking his gear, he began to check rigging straps, stirrup leather, latigo and cinch straps for signs of wear and strain. All were asked to bear unusual tension in trick riding as he shifted his weight from side to side. Later, he finished out the day by grooming the Ovaro and then led the horse to the water trough at the far side of the main tent. Dusk had settled in when he returned, tethered the horse, and stepped into his wagon. He halted, surprise flooding his face.

"*Zdrahvstvootie,* Fargo," Galina said with a wide smile that didn't quite disguise the hint of a smirk in it.

Nicholas and Viktor were beside her, and two burly cowhands stood behind Viktor. "You are surprised, yes?" she added with a low half laugh.

"I sure am," Fargo admitted, and Galina stepped forward and linked her arm in his.

"You see, you are not the only one who can follow a trail. Your spectacular horse made it almost easy," she said.

"You have done very well, Fargo. You were worth every cent we paid you," Nicholas put in. "You have found the egg. Now you can go on your way. *Spasibo*."

Fargo felt the sudden surge of concern for Tanya sweep through him. This was a ruthless pursuit. A line of deaths was proof of that. He didn't want her to be another casualty. "No, not so fast. I haven't found it. I'm not sure it's even here," he said.

"We are sure. It all fits. They will need time and a safe place to keep it," Nicholas said. "We'll take it from here."

"I'd like to see it through alone. It'd be better. I can get her to listen to me," Fargo said.

"Little Tanya? Listen to you? I don't think so, Fargo," Galina smiled.

"I don't think she's really part of it. They're using her," Fargo said.

"Using her?" Galina put in, her tone chiding. "I do believe little Tanya has carved a place in Fargo's heart."

"I just don't want to see anybody else killed. I want to be sure," Fargo said.

"We are sure," Nicholas said flatly.

Fargo's eyes took in the man and Galina. "You know Tanya?"

"Not personally, but she was part of the Moscow circus for a while, and we know some of the people she has been seen with," Nicholas said.

"And they're thieves?"

"Thieves, troublemakers, peasant scum."

"Let me finish the job," Fargo said. "I'll get the egg is it's here."

"We'll finish it," Nicholas said.

"You can't strong-arm her here in the middle of the circus. Everybody here sticks together," Fargo said.

"Circus people. We know that," Nicholas said. "We'll get her out of here. Then she'll give us the egg or tell us where it is. She'll talk."

Fargo swore silently as he decided not to argue further. But his concern for Tanya had increased. He'd have to get to her and tell her she was in danger, make her believe him. "When do you figure to take her?" he questioned.

"After her performance. If we try to take her before, she might see us and run. After her performance she'll be relaxed. We'll move quickly, before she gets back to her wagon," Nicholas said. He snapped his fingers at the two burly cowhands, and they suddenly had their six-guns out and pointed at Fargo.

"Nicholas is thinking what I am, Fargo," Galina said, a touch of sadness in her voice. "Listening to you, we are afraid we can't trust you at the moment. You seem sympathetic to little Tanya."

"It's not that," Fargo protested. "I told you, I'd like to finish it without more killing."

"We can't afford compassion, my friend," Galina said, and Fargo's eyes narrowed at her.

"I keep wondering if this is the simple robbery you painted it to be," he said.

"Of course it is," Galina said.

"It will be something for you to wonder about in the years to come. We want you to have those years," Nicholas said, delivering the veiled threat with avuncular concern. One of the two cowhands took the Colt from him while the other kept the six-gun trained on his chest. "Tie him," Nicholas said firmly, and the two cowhands began to use a length of lariat twine to tie his hands behind his back and his ankles together. When they finished, they pushed him onto the bed. Nicholas and Viktor started toward the door, and Galina paused, her lips pursed as she met Fargo's gaze.

"I figured a different ending for you and me," he said.

"So did I," Galina said with an imperious gaze. "But life is full of disappointments."

"True enough. I just wish I could be sure who I ought to be disappointed in," he returned.

"You may never know that answer, Fargo," Galina said smugly as she patted his cheek with one hand. She paused at the door with a glance at the two cowhands. "Meet us in an hour. You know where," she said and hurried out. Fargo's eyes went to the two men as they sat down to wait.

"How'd you boys get into this?" he asked.

"We got hired. Real good money," the one said and laughed. His face was fleshy and he had a small scar on his upper lip, Fargo noticed.

"Let me go and I'll get you more money," Fargo said.

"You have it on you?" the other one asked, too quickly.

"No," Fargo said. He knew their type. If he said yes, they'd simply take the money and leave him tied. "But I can get it real quick," he offered.

"Forget it, cousin," the scarred-lip one snorted.

"How'd they hire you?" Fargo queried.

"At a bar. Viktor hired us," the one said. "We never met any Russians before."

"Look, this could be bigger than you think. You don't know what you're into," Fargo said.

"I got the idea you don't either," the one said, and Fargo swore inwardly at the truth in the answer. "Besides, we don't give a shit," the man said.

"I mean, maybe you should be getting more money," Fargo tried. "There's been a half-dozen people killed on this thing."

"We figure to do any killing that has to be done," scar-lip said and leaned over to turn the lamp on low as night descended and the interior of the wagon grew dim.

Fargo tugged at the ropes on his wrists behind his back and found no slack in them. He lay on his side, knees drawn half up, and cursed time. It always seemed to go too slowly or too quickly, depending on its own malicious will. Now it was moving much too quickly and the hour seemed to fly by. The two men rose and started for the door and the fleshy one paused to glance back at him. He half-drew the Colt from his belt as he stared back. "Maybe we ought to knock him out," he said.

"Why not?" the other agreed. The man started toward him, the Colt in his hand now held by the barrel. Fargo drew his legs up, measured seconds and distance, and as the man reached the edge of the bed and lifted his arm to bring the gun butt down, Fargo kicked out with both his bound-together feet. The blow hit the man's abdomen and he fell backwards with a curse, landing on one knee, with pain showing in the redness of his face.

"Son of a bitch," he cursed and raised the gun to fire, but the other one grabbed his arm.

"No, for Christ's sake. No shooting," he said. "God knows who that'd bring."

"One of you has some sense," Fargo taunted as the scarred-lip one rose to his feet and stuck the Colt back into his belt.

"I'll be back for you," he said as the other one tugged at his arm.

"They're expecting us. Let's go, dammit," the second one said, and Fargo watched both disappear out the door, slamming it shut after them.

Fargo instantly rolled from the bed and grimaced in pain as he landed hard on the floor. The show would be starting now. He could hear the opening strains from the band ever so faintly inside the wagon. Rolling to his knees, he managed to push himself upwards and balanced there precariously on his bound-together feet. He started to hop toward the door, fell, and had to take precious time to pull himself upright again. He managed to stay up for two more bounces and fell to his knees only an arm's length from the door. Again he pulled himself upright, but this time, turning his shoulder forward, he flung himself against the door. It didn't budge and he swore aloud. With his ankles bound together he couldn't get enough force to knock the door open, and he fell back onto his back, rolling onto his side as his gaze swept the room from where he lay.

He sought something sharp on which he could cut the wrist ropes, but he found nothing. The bedstand rested flat against the floor; no sharp edges came from the baseboards; the chipped dresser offered nothing. His eyes paused on the kerosene lamp. The shattered glass might provide a piece large enough to cut the ropes with. But he discarded the idea, aware that he'd never be able to shatter the glass without spilling kerosene and setting the place on fire. The porcelain pitcher atop the dresser came into his sight next, and he rolled across the floor, pulled himself up against the dresser, and, swiveling his head, knocked the pitcher to the floor.

It shattered into pieces and he dropped down at once,

found the largest piece, and maneuvered himself around until he could grasp it with his fingers. Holding the length of jagged porcelain in his fingers, he began to saw it back and forth across his wrist ropes. He could hear the band playing the music for the sword swallower. Tanya would go on next. Galina, Nicholas, and the others were already positioned to get to her when the performance was over, he knew, his fingers already starting to cramp. He halted, flexed his fingers to bring some life back into them, and began sawing against the sliver of porcelain. He stopped minutes later. His fingers had stiffened, but that wasn't the reason he stopped. It would take too long, he realized. They'd be off and gone with Tanya and he'd still be sawing away at the ropes. There wasn't much time left, and he cursed bitterly as he dropped the sliver of porcelain from his fingers and rolled across the floor.

He had to get out. Perhaps he'd find something outside sharp enough to slash the ropes. He had to get out. Moving onto his back, almost at the door, he drew his bound-together legs back, tightened his every muscle, and kicked out with all his strength, smashing both feet into the door. It shuddered but still held. He drew his legs back again and kicked out once more, driving both feet hard against the door. It shuddered again and he saw a crack appear near the lock. Positioning himself on his back again, he kicked out one more time, every last bit of his calf, knee, and thigh muscle in it. The door gave way, smashing open with the sound of splintering wood, and Fargo heard the opening bars of Tanya's music.

Arms still behind his back, ankles still bound together, he flung himself forward out of the wagon and fell onto the ground, wincing with pain as he landed on a hard place. Tanya's music was in full sound now. She was into her performance as, cursing, Fargo rolled himself across the ground. The tents seemed terribly far away as he continued to roll. He had traveled another fifty feet when he saw the figure moving toward him and called out. It was a young boy, one of the circus hangers-on he'd seen before. "Help me," Fargo said. "Untie these damn ropes behind my back."

"Jesus, what happened to you, mister?" the boy asked as he knelt down and began to work on the wrist ropes.

"Somebody's idea of a joke," Fargo explained. "Faster, please, son."

"I'm trying. They're tied real tight," the boy said, and in what seemed like an hour later but was only some thirty seconds, Fargo felt the wrist ropes part and quickly brought his arms around to untie the ankle ropes himself.

"Thanks, son," he flung back as he rose and raced off. He rounded the tent to the back where the performers gathered and edged to the front to scan the audience. He spotted one of the cowhands in the first row near the side of the tent, then the other one with the scarred lip alongside the entrance flap. He scanned the audience again. Galina, Nicholas, and Viktor were not to be seen, which meant they were waiting outside someplace while the hired guns were positioned to watch from inside.

"Where the hell have you been?" The voice cut into his concentration and he saw Jim Kelly bearing down on him. "Where's your horse? You're on next," the circus master roared.

"Not tonight," Fargo said, and Kelly's face grew red as Fargo didn't look at him.

"You cancel out like this and you're through, Fargo," Kelly threatened.

"Your call," Fargo said, still not looking at the man. His eyes were on Tanya. She was high on the trapeze, sailing through the air from one to the other with consummate grace and ease. She had added a small ruffle around the waist of her skintight leotard, he saw. His eyes riveted on her, he watched her sail through the air, catch hold of the next hanging trapeze, and use her legs to move the trapeze faster and faster through the air.

Suddenly he saw her let go of the trapeze, her small body going through the air in a high arc, away from the other trapezes, sailing to where there'd be only the tent poles, the tent, and the bone-shattering ground to stop her. "No . . . ah, no, goddammit," Fargo bit out, his lips pulled back, his thoughts filled with Pavlev's willingness to sacrifice himself in a last desperate act and Dmitri's suicide. "No, not again," he murmured.

9

He watched, beyond comprehending, beyond understanding, bitterness enveloping him to make him feel almost sick with despair. Then suddenly he felt his mouth fall open and his eyes grow wide. As the slender shape somersaulted through the air to her apparent shattering death, the side tent flaps were being pulled open. Tanya catapulted through the opening at the end of her arc and he saw the hay wagon just beyond the opened tent flaps. He felt something close to a cheer well up inside him as she landed in the hay wagon, sending up a small shower of hay.

It hadn't been one more sacrifice, one more suicidal gesture beyond his understanding. She reappeared in the hay wagon, climbed over the side, and leaped onto the horse standing alongside. She was racing away as he turned and started to run from the tent to where he had left the Ovaro. He skidded to a halt as he saw the line of figures form to block his way: roustabouts, the Risselli brothers, Ahmed the sword swallower, more roustabouts. He understood at once. All members of the circus family, they'd been alerted and rallied to help one of their own. No questions asked, the bond was all that was needed.

"Let me through," Fargo told them. "You don't understand. I want to help her." But the line of figures didn't move and he reached for his Colt to fire a shot for effect, only to remember that his gun was gone. He turned and ran the way he'd come, through the main tent, glancing back to see the line still standing, uncertain what to do next. He raced out the other side, past wagons to where the Ovaro was tethered. He reached the horse just as Leonid pushed to his feet. He had hobbled the horse, Fargo saw, tying ropes from foreleg to rear leg. It'd take another five precious minutes to untie the ropes. Cutting them loose would leave the ends dangling, long enough to trip up the horse.

"You damn fool," Fargo spat at the man as he knelt down and started to untie the hobbles. "They're here, dammit. It's not me you ought to be worrying about." He saw Leonid's stolid face frown, uncertainty creeping into it.

"Who's here?" the man questioned.

"Nicholas Rhesnev, his man Viktor, Galina, and some hired guns," Fargo flung back as he continued to untie the hobbles.

"Oh, my God. You brought them," Leonid said, his voice a hoarse whisper.

"I didn't bring them. They followed me," Fargo said as he undid the last of the hobbles and climbed into the saddle. "I'm going after them."

"I'll go with you. I'll get a horse," Leonid said.

"You'll only slow me down," Fargo said.

Leonid stared at him. "Tanya told me you'd come to get the egg, you were in their pay. Why do you do this now? Who are you?"

"I'm not sure I know," Fargo tossed back as he sent the pinto into a gallop, leaving the man and the tents behind in seconds. A half-moon gave more than enough light to ride, but he had to slow to a walk to discern tracks. There were too many prints on the road, but he spotted two sets of hoofprints that turned into the low hills. They were likely those of the two hired guns. That meant Galina, Nicholas, and Viktor were ahead of them, and somewhere still further ahead was Tanya. He paused and studied the two sets of prints he trailed. The horses were almost at a walk, their riders having a hard time following a trail in the night. He moved forward slowly as he became convinced the two men would halt and continue the trail in the morning.

The hoofprints crested a rise in the land and moved through a space heavily bordered by mountain ash. He reined to a halt as he heard the low snort of a horse perhaps a hundred yards ahead. Dropping to the ground, he moved forward on foot through the soft cover of rabbitbrush. He left the Ovaro a dozen paces behind and crept forward, the dark bulk of the two horses appearing first. He circled around the horses to see the two sleeping figures, both men dressed, resting their heads on their saddles. He crept closer and recognized the nearest of the two, not by his scarred lip—it was too dark for that—but by the Colt stuck in his belt.

Drawing the thin, double-edged throwing knife from its calf holster, Fargo crept toward the sleeping figures. It was the second man he had to be prepared for, he knew, and on feet silent as a cougar's pads, he reached the nearest man. Carefully positioning himself, he dropped to one knee, cast a glance at the second man asleep some dozen yards away, and marked the spot in his mind. Holding the knife in his left hand, he yanked the Colt from the man's belt. The man awoke instantly. "What the hell . . . ?" he half-yelled as he started to sit up and felt the tip of the knife against his throat.

"Don't move," Fargo hissed, and the Colt in his right

hand was already turning toward the second man, who had snapped awake and sat up. Fargo saw him draw his gun as he let out a curse. The Colt barked once and the man's figure jerked violently as he fell sideways and then lay still. "Damn fool," Fargo said. "But then I expected he'd be." Keeping the tip of the knife against scarred-lip's face, he drew the man's gun from its holster and moved back. "Now, you going to be a damn fool, too?" he asked.

"No, sir," the man said.

"Now tell me what Rhesnev told you," Fargo said.

"Not much. He hired us as backup. He never told us why or what for."

The answer fit. Rhesnev wouldn't have told them much. "You were supposed to help them get the girl after the performance tonight," he said, and the man nodded. "Where were they going to take her?" Fargo asked.

"I don't know. Once they had her we were finished," the man said. "They were going to pay us off and we'd be on our way."

Fargo grunted unnhappily. The answer held little hope for Tanya. No witnesses to anything. No one at the finish but Nicholas, Viktor, and Galina. But they were wrong. They'd have company. He emptied the man's gun of bullets and handed it back to him. "Give me your gunbelt," he said, and the man obeyed, watching him empty the cartridges from it. "Now you're going to hightail it back to wherever you came from. Come after me and it'll be your last ride."

"I won't be back," the man said, and Fargo watched him saddle his horse and ride away, convinced he was fearful enough to keep riding. Fargo called the Ovaro to him and swung onto the horse. Riding slowly so as not to miss a mark, he finally came upon the three sets of hoofprints. The prints were close together. They were also riding slowly so they'd not miss Tanya's trail. Fargo picked out a set of prints from her horse after a half hour, largely trampled by the other hoofmarks. She hadn't slowed and the trail led deeper into thickly forested hill country. He had the feeling she was fleeing aimlessly, fearfully, not running *to* anything, but simply away from him.

That much had become clear. Leonid hadn't been aware Galina and the others were on hand. Tanya wouldn't have known, either. She was fleeing him, afraid that perhaps he had been hired to do more than retrieve the egg. He continued to ride slowly, saw where Galina and the others had halted to rest, and pressed on as the dawn finally slid across the sky with long fingers of pink. He increased his pace as the tracks became easier to spot and the trail widened, a moose path through the forest of blue spruce and canyon oak. He had ridden another hour, the sun fully out and warm, when he reined to a halt as he heard the sound of voices. Turning the Ovaro into the trees, he edged uphill as he rode forward and halted when he saw Galina, Nicholas, and Viktor below. A fourth horse stood nibbling a patch of wild strawberries to one side.

Galina and the two men were arguing angrily in Russian, and though he could understand nothing they said, he quickly realized what had happened from their gestures and Galina's explosive behavior as she paced back and forth, her eyes searching the ground. The horse was the one Tanya had used, but Tanya had left it to go forward on foot. But the others had found no footprints. Fargo felt the frown touch his brow. Maybe Tanya had gone into the trees on foot and they hadn't the experience to pick up her trail. Suddenly Galina whirled on Nicholas and Viktor and spoke in English.

"No. No, no, no. She didn't go on. She turned back. She left the horse to confuse us and turned back," Galina said and pulled herself onto her horse. "There is no trail. She turned back, I tell you."

Nicholas shrugged and there was concession in the gesture. He climbed onto his horse and Viktor pulled himself onto his mount. Fargo stayed in the trees and watched them slowly retrace their steps, this time making sorties into the trees every few yards. Fargo waited till they were out of sight before he edged the pinto downward to where Tanya's horse continued to enjoy the wild strawberries. Dismounting, Fargo's eyes scanned the path. Galina had been right. There was no trail along the path, not a solitary footprint. Fargo smiled as he stepped into the treeline, searching the ground in all directions and finally emerging to go into the trees on the other side of the wide path. Again he searched the ground, moving in every direction, and when he returned to the Ovaro his brow held a deep furrow.

He led the Ovaro down the moose trail, peering at the edges where the witchgrass grew thick enough to hide footprints from anyone but a trailsman. But he found no sign of a footprint and he halted after another few hundred yards, the frown deeper into his forehead. It didn't make sense that she'd double back, thinking that he'd be in pursuit and knowing he had trailed her to the circus. But she'd left the horse and seemed to vanish. Only no one vanishes just like that, he frowned. Yet if she hadn't doubled back, and hadn't left any footprints, what had she done, dammit, he pondered. A movement caught his eye and he looked up to see a horned lark wing from the branches. He stared at it, watched it light on another branch and then take wing again, and he felt the small smile begin to touch his lips.

"I'll be damned," he murmured. "Of course. Trapeze to trees. It would be duck soup for her." He sent the pinto forward, and this time his eyes scanned the branches, spotted a small twig broken off at one point, leaves torn at another. She had made her way swinging from branch to branch, and he felt genuine admiration for her inventiveness. But he knew she couldn't be making much time and she'd have to stop to rest often enough. He sent the pinto into a fast canter down the wide trail. He knew the reason for the ruffled waistband on her leotard now. It concealed a pouch where she had the egg. He was still admiring her cleverness when he spotted the slender shape in the trees ahead and saw her turn at the sound of the horse, startled surprise on her face.

She dropped to the ground as he rode to a halt, and the surprise had turned into weariness and defeat as she silently faced him. She flexed her arms and rubbed her biceps as he dismounted. "You win. You are very good," she said. "You found me the first time. Now you have done it again."

"I came to help you, Tanya," he said. "I don't want to see you killed for that damn egg."

"But you are here. You chased after me. You were hired to get the egg, no matter what the price," Tanya said.

"I'm not talking about me. The others are after you. They followed me to the circus," he said, and her eyes widened a fraction as she stared at him. "Nicholas Rhesnev and his man, Viktor and Galina."

Tanya's eyes grew large. "Rhesnev is here? Galina, too?"

"Yes," Fargo said. "You've outfoxed them for the moment, but they will keep looking for you."

"This is a big country. We thought we could hide here until we were ready," Tanya said.

"Ready to make a deal and sell it," Fargo said.

"Sell it? Is that what they told you this was about? Selling the egg?"

"Yes. I understand it'd bring a damn fancy price," Fargo said.

"It would," Tanya agreed. "And you think you've been chasing a band of common thieves?"

"I started out thinking that, then I began to wonder. I didn't know. Suppose you tell me what this is all about," he said.

Wariness crept into her eyes at once. "If you'll help me get away from them," she said. He frowned at her as her request revolved in his mind. He didn't break deals or go back on his word and he'd given his word to find the egg. But he suddenly remembered something he'd let slip by. Rhesnev had dismissed him. *Now you can go your way. Spasibo,* the man had said. There was no promise left. The deal was over. He was free to do whatever he wished. But he'd be damned if he'd commit himself to Tanya without knowing more.

"Even if I helped you get away this time, they'll keep coming after you. I'm sure of that. They'll hire somebody else to find you," he told her.

"I think not like you," she said. "We'll find another place to hide in this big country."

"No promises," Fargo said. "I know you have the egg with you. Tell me about it."

"You don't know that," she resisted.

"Under those ruffles someplace," he said. "You going to talk or do I just walk away?"

She let a deep sigh of weariness escape her, and he saw the turmoil of emotions in her eyes as she reached a hand under the ruffles around her waist. She pulled a beaded pouch forward, opened the top, and brought out the jeweled egg. Fargo stared at it, the beauty of it almost overwhelming: shimmering green-gold enamel crossed with lines of red-gold enamel; the rubies, emeralds, and sapphires imbedded in it in a crisscross pattern, and the base of matched pearls a shining white contrast. The entire object seemed to vibrate with beauty and craftsmanship. "It is magnificent, isn't it?" Tanya said as she held it up for him. "Fabergé and his craftsmen are the very best."

"I've never seen anything like it, that's for sure," Fargo said.

"There isn't anything like these Easter eggs of jewels and craftsmanship Fabergé has begun to make for the czar. But they are more than meets the eye. Each has a little secret or surprise inside it. Sometimes it is a perfectly detailed coach, sometimes a picture of the czarina, sometimes a flower made of platinum, agate, and amyethyst, but always something. This one contains something ordered by the czar himself."

She turned the egg, pressed a tiny snap at the rear, and the egg opened into two halves kept together by tiny jeweled hinges. Inside the egg he saw a miniature, tightly coiled scroll made of gold, covered with lines of names engraved into the gold, unreadable except through a magnifying glass. It was all a breathtaking example of the jeweler's art, he realized.

"Remember when I told you of life for the ordinary peasant villager under the czar?" Tanya asked. "The demands, the raids by his cossacks, the carrying off of whatever young woman takes their fancy, the cruelty of the tax collectors? You asked why the people have never protested or tried to fight back, and do you remember what I told you?"

"You said the czar has someone in his pay in every village or region who keeps him and his generals informed of anyone trying to make trouble," Fargo said.

"That's right. This little gold scroll is the master list of every one of those people, every one of the czar's village and regional spies," Tanya said. "He thought putting it inside one of Fabergé's eggs would be the perfect place to keep it hidden, and he would have been right except for one thing."

"What was that?" Fargo inquired.

"One of the craftsmen who worked on it in the Bolshaya Morskaya Street shop in St. Petersburg was dismissed after a very unpleasant disagreement. He told one of our people about the scroll that was being made to put inside the egg."

"Our people?" Fargo queried.

"There is a group of us who want to overthrow the czar. That is the only way the Russian people will ever get out of his yoke. We knew that if we had this scroll we'd know who the czar's spies were in every region. We'd be able to deal with them and finally get a revolution started. We'd know the names and faces of the czar's people who have stopped every attempt at the people organizing to revolt. When we had the egg stolen we had already decided to bring it here to America. We knew it would take us perhaps a year to analyze all those names and decipher the code for each village and region."

"I'll be damned," Fargo breathed.

"Everything was planned very carefully, for a long time. There were those who were charged with stealing the egg and those given the responsibility of getting it out of Russia. Leonid and I came to America six months ago to establish a safe place to keep the egg."

"You didn't think they'd be coming after you?" Fargo asked.

"Of course we did, but we hoped it would take them a long time to trace things to America. It seems we were wrong about that," Tanya said.

"You sure were," Fargo commented.

"In any venture there are always those who can be bought," Tanya said.

"But not Pavlev, not the one called Dmitri, and not some of the others," Fargo said.

"No, they all knew this was our chance to free Russia of the czar and his generals. Pavlev was our leader, but we all knew this was a chance we'd never have again."

It all made sense now as Fargo listened to her. The words he had heard used—dedication, traitor, the self-sacrifice that hadn't fit the picture of common thieves—it was suddenly all clear, and he studied Tanya as she stood before him. Behind her diminutive, jewellike presence he saw the dedicated steel, and he had to admire her even as he felt concern for her.

"Where did you think you were going with the egg, dressed like that?" he asked.

"I have some money in the pouch. I intended to buy proper clothes at the first town," she said. "Then there are some people in Portland. I will contact them—if you will help me."

"I'll make a bargain with you," he said. "I'll help you if you promise you'll give them the egg. I won't help you hang onto it and keep putting your life in danger."

Tanya's eyes searched his, her face grave. "I think that is the nicest thing anyone has ever said to me," she said.

"Maybe I just don't want your neck on my conscience," he said gruffly.

"That doesn't change what I just said," Tanya

answered, and still holding the egg in one hand, she stepped forward and pressed her lips to his. "It is still *spasibo* . . . thank you." Her lips pressed his again, soft strength, sensory promises. She stepped back and carefully put the jeweled egg back into the pouch beneath the ruffles. He climbed onto the Ovaro and swung her up in front of him. She leaned back, her small, tight rear resting against his crotch and her lithe strength touching his chest.

"Now I understand why you couldn't tell me whether you'd be going back to Russia," he told her as he let the horse trot along the path.

"Whatever I do, I must get word to Leonid and have him meet me somewhere. He has been a good friend and a good ally," Tanya said. Fargo rode on to where the path grew thin and began to turn downward out of the low hills, then suddenly reined to a halt, a realization coming around to push at him. "You never answered me back there, about giving these people in Portland the egg. I don't take you an inch further until you answer that," he said.

"I could love someone like you, Fargo," she said.

"Good, but that's no answer, dammit," he snapped.

"I promise," she said. "We have a saying in Russia. To find a good lover is wonderful. To find a good friend is wonderful. But to find someone who is a good friend and a good lover is best of all. I think you are best of all."

He hugged her with one arm and sent the Ovaro downhill, found a road that led to a small town, and halted at the edge of the town. "Stay here," he said as he slid from the horse and went into the town. He found a general store where he bought a pair of small ladies' riding britches and two blouses. Tanya was beside the pinto when he returned. She stepped behind a big hackberry and changed into the new clothes. They fit her lithe slenderness a little loosely, but she still managed to look as jewellike as the egg. She kept the pouch around her waist, he noticed as they rode on.

Dusk came soon and he found a spot beside two fragrant Norway spruces as he turned from the road, dismounted, and unsaddled the horse. "I am very tired," Tanya said. "My arms are still sore from going through the trees."

"Only a trapeze artist could have done it," Fargo said. "I'm pretty much played out, too. Didn't get any sleep last night."

"Because of me," she said and sat down on the bedroll he rolled out. They ate some cold beef jerky he had in his saddlebag, and she undressed with him and curled up in his arms, putting the pouch alongside her.

"We'll make up for it tomorrow night," she told him, her face against his chest.

"Maybe tomorrow morning," he said and heard her tiny giggle. She was asleep in moments. He closed his eyes, very aware that sleep was a welcome friend.

He felt the warmth of the morning sun when day came, but let himself sleep a little longer, Tanya a clinging little form half across his chest. When he woke again it was the voice that woke him. He thought it was Tanya but then realized it was not and snapped his eyes open.

"How charming," the voice said, and the tall blond-haired figure came into focus, an arch to the blond eyebrows. Tanya awoke then, pushing partly away from him as she turned on her back. Fargo sat up, aware of the disdain in Galina's eyes as she stared at him and Tanya. Flanking her, he saw Viktor and Nicholas, both men grim-faced. Fargo reached out for his trousers. "Be careful, Fargo," Galina said, and he saw her draw the pistol from the waistband of her riding britches.

"Just putting my pants on, honey. It'll help you relax," Fargo said and saw the fire flash in Galina's deep brown eyes.

"Watch your tongue," she hissed as he lifted his buttocks and drew on his trousers. The Colt in its holster lay some six feet from him, but he knew the kind of accurate shot Galina was and he moved carefully.

"One for you," he said to Galina. "Didn't expect you to be along."

"We came onto the body of one of the hands we hired. We realized it had to have been your work, and we knew that you were also following."

"So you turned back and picked up my tracks," Fargo said.

"Yes, the lone set of hoofprints on the trail where we turned off," Nicholas put in. "You were not fooled as we were. Why? Indulge an old man's curiosity."

"There are foxes and there are butterflies," Fargo said and enjoyed Rhesnev's frown.

"Give us the egg," Galina cut in sharply, and Tanya, still beautifully naked, took his arm. Galina's smile was made of icy disdain. "It's quite amazing how peasants are attracted to peasants," she said.

"You've a short memory, honey," Fargo said and saw Galina's lips thin.

"Give us the egg," she snapped.

"I don't have it," Tanya said.

Galina ignored the answer and her eyes swept the bedroll, halting as they came to the pouch. She stepped forward and Fargo felt Tanya's hands tighten on his arm as Galina stooped and scooped up the pouch. She pulled it open and her hand emerged holding the egg. "*Da!*" she said triumphantly.

"No," Tanya screamed, and Fargo saw her fly from beside him, catapulting herself through the air. Out of the corner of his eye he saw her tear the egg from Galina as she dove past her. But he was rolling across the ground, his hand closing around the handle of the Colt as he yanked it from the holster. He came up on one knee to see Tanya with the jeweled egg in her hand, Galina with the pistol trained on her.

"Give me the egg, you little fool," Galina said.

"No," Tanya said, and Fargo saw the fervent desperation in her eyes. Nicholas and Viktor were watching her and Galina.

"I'll kill you then," Galina said.

"No," Fargo said, and Nicholas and Viktor flicked their eyes to him.

Galina's eyes stayed on Tanya, the pistol leveled at the slender form. "Tell her I don't miss, Fargo," Galina said, not shifting her eyes.

"You know I don't miss, either, Galina," he said.

"Then neither of us will miss," Galina said, her voice firm, and Fargo's eyes went from Galina to Tanya and back to Galina again. In Galina's face he saw implacable determination mixed with contempt, in Tanya's the unswerving idealism of those who believe. Damn them both, he swore inwardly. Damn them for drawing him into it. Tanya was trembling, he saw, yet too dedicated to back down. Damn martyrs, he thought. Galina held the final ace, and she was too committed and too imperious to back down. He swore again silently and knew he couldn't let it go down to its deadly end, only seconds away now.

He brought the barrel of the Colt down an inch and his

eyes were riveted on Galina's finger against the trigger of her pistol. He saw the almost imperceptible tightening of the skin around her knuckle and he fired the Colt, a split second before she pulled the trigger of her pistol. His bullet hit her gun just as she fired and her shot went wild as the gun tore from her hand. He heard Tanya scream, but it was a cry of anguish not pain, and out of the corner of his eye he saw the jeweled egg explode into a thousand gleaming pieces, a dazzling shower of gold, green, red, and white.

Galina cursed in Russian as she held her hand, more numbed than injured, but Fargo saw Viktor yanking the heavy pistol from beneath his jacket. Diving forward, Fargo stayed low as Viktor brought the gun up to fire at him and sailed into the man's legs. Viktor fell backwards and his shot went into the air. Fargo leaped, came down on him, and forced the man's gun hand backwards as he drove his elbow into Viktor's abdomen. Fargo heard Viktor's gasp of breath as he brought a short, chopping uppercut upwards and Viktor went limp, the gun falling from his hand. Fargo rose to his feet, the Colt still in his hand, and saw Nicholas beside Galina.

"That's all," he barked. "No more shit." His eyes went to Tanya where she sat, cross-legged and naked on the ground, tears falling from her eyes as she gathered up tiny bits and slivers of the egg. He strode to her, scooped up her blouse and put it over her. Viktor had come around and was pushing himself to his feet as he wiped a hand across his chin. "It's over, for all of you," Fargo said angrily, his eyes pinpointing Galina.

"Am I supposed to thank you?" she sniffed.

"No. I don't want anybody's thanks," Fargo said. "But you can go back now."

"Empty-handed," Galina sniffed.

"That's right, no egg. But they don't have it, either. That's what you really wanted, wasn't it?" he said. Galina didn't reply, but he saw the admission in her eyes. "This Fabergé dude can make the czar another jeweled egg. No scroll inside this time. It'll be safer that way," he said dryly, and Galina turned away. She walked to where he saw the three horses, and Viktor and Nicholas followed. She climbed onto her horse and Viktor followed on his, Nicholas close behind. "Drop me a postcard," Fargo called after them and turned to where Tanya still sat amid the shattered jeweled egg.

She lifted her eyes to him as he knelt on one knee beside her. The tears had stopped but the pain and defeat stayed in her face. "We failed," she said. "We failed. There is nowhere to go from here. This was our one chance."

"Other chances will come along," he said.

She shook her head despondently. "No," she said. "The scroll was the key to all our plans. Without it, we are nothing again. You can't understand how terrible that is."

"You're alive," he said. "I understand that and that's not at all terrible."

"No, no, that's wonderful," she said as her arms rose to encircle his neck. "I will never forget you for that. Nor for a lot of other things."

He lifted her up and deposited her on the Ovaro. "Let's celebrate being alive," he said, and she nodded, slender, lithe legs protruding from under the blouse that hung open from around her shoulders. After gathering up his bedroll, he swung onto the horse with her and rode deeper into the spruce, where he found a still and shaded spot filled with the fragrance of wild, living things. Tanya came to him on the soft forest bed, and once again her lovemaking combined her own special acrobatics with her own special passion. When her final scream of ecstasy died away, he lay beside her.

She finally rose on one elbow to peer at him. "What are you thinking?" she asked.

He smiled. "I was thinking I did something few men ever get a chance to do. I changed the course of history," he said.

She thought for a moment. "Yes," she said. "Or perhaps you only delayed it."

"That'll do," he said. "That'll do."

"I guess it will have to, for both of us," she said and clung to him as if she'd be there forever.

LOOKING FORWARD!
The following is the opening section from the next novel in the exciting *Trailsman* series from Signet:

THE TRAILSMAN #157
GHOST RANCH MASSACRE

The vast Hopi Lands, 1860,
In what will be Arizona,
Where magic is real
And an ancient spirit returns for revenge

"No! No! Please don't!" she screamed, her dark eyes wide with terror. Above her stood the black-caped man, a long, glittering sword in his hand. He plunged it downward and she shrieked.

"Don't! Don't! It's really hurting me!"

He took up another and drove it in horizontally, while she screamed again, a jeweled studded slipper slipping off her foot as she jerked in agony.

"Please! Please stop!"

Skye Fargo watched as the man drove a third blade through the coffin-shaped box and into the body of the ebony-haired woman locked inside with only her head and feet protruding. She moaned. The sound died in her throat and her head fell to one side.

"Oh, it is terrible, is it not?" the magician said in a liquid, accented voice as he advanced toward the footlights. He swirled the cape about him, and his huge protruding black eyes seemed to look into the faces of each member of the audience. "To see the beautiful Arabella die such a horrible death! What a frightful loss! But I, Magnus the Magnificent, I have learned the secrets of life and death, the ancient mysteries from the line of Zoroaster . . ."

Fargo smiled to himself. It was a damned good trick. It really looked as though the long swords had gone right through the woman's body. As the magician prattled on, Fargo's eyes swept the stage and he saw, beneath the box, the slow dripping of red blood. A pool was gathering on the floor below. Several others noticed it too.

"She's really dead!" a woman cried out.

"The blood! She's bleeding!" a man in the first row shouted at the magician. The man, wearing overalls and a straw hat, stood up and pointed anxiously.

Magnus the Magnificent refused to look and only waved the man down, as if not believing him, and continued to talk hocus pocus. The audience grew restless with tension. Several more men jumped to their feet and shouted at the magician. But Magnus ignored them and continued to try to speak over the babble. A woman in a bonnet sitting near Fargo sobbed into her handkerchief.

Fargo began to wonder if something really *had* gone wrong with the trick. He stared at the box onstage and at the dark-haired beauty named Arabella. Her lovely face was turned toward the audience, eyes closed, long black hair flowing down to the ground. Fargo kept his gaze on her and then saw the barest twitch of an eyelid and the flare of her nostrils as she took a breath. She was alive, he thought, relieved. So, the dripping red liquid was just another part of the trick. He smiled to himself. It was a damned good show.

The audience was in a near riot now, most of them standing and stamping their feet, trying to get the magician to turn around and look. The pooled fake blood beneath the box began to run in a rivulet down the raked stage toward the footlights. Just then Magnus paused in his speech and glanced down. He did a double-take as he saw the trickling red blood, and his face took on an expression of horror.

"Oh, my God!" he shrieked. Magnus whirled about and advanced upstage to look at the blood under the box. He paced, wrung his hands, and tore at his mass of wild gray hair as if in helpless despair. The audience went wild. Women cried and men were on their feet shouting for a doctor and waving their hats in the air. Suddenly Magnus snapped back toward the audience and held up his hands with a grand gesture. The theater fell silent.

"This is a terrible tragedy," Magnus said, a sob catching in his sonorous voice. "Such a terrible thing has never happened to me before."

Yeah, not since the last show, Fargo thought to himself with a grin. The magician laid his hand on the wooden box and bowed his head. Several women sniffled.

"Murderer! Arrest him!" a man shouted.

"Wait!" Magnus said, raising his large head. "There is but one hope! One small possibility . . ." The audience was hanging on his every word. Magnus drew a small glass vial from his cape and held it up. "The elixir of life, three drops of this precious fluid which was given to me by Zarcon of Arabia. I hope it will be enough."

Magnus intoned some magic words, waved the tiny bottle over the wooden box, then unstoppered it and poured the contents over the top. A loud explosion followed by a puff of red smoke made everyone in the small theater jump. When the smoke had cleared, Magnus began pulling the swords slowly out of the box as the audience held its breath. Then Magnus snapped his fingers in front of the woman's face, and she opened her eyes and smiled.

"Where am I?" Arabella said, as if confused. "I was having a dream about some angels . . ."

The audience broke out into frenzied applause and relieved laughter as Magnus unlocked the box and helped her out. Arabella jumped down, retrieved her slipper, and took a bow. Fargo admired again her tiny hourglass figure in the tight red-sequined costume and the way the color set off the smooth skin of her deep cleavage and waving ebony hair. He wondered if she was busy after the show.

Magnus and Arabella disappeared behind the red curtain, and Frederico the Fantastical Conjuror, a red-mustached man in a blue silk turban, appeared and performed some card tricks, pulled chickens out of empty barrels, and made bouquets of flowers appear out of nowhere. All the while Frederico kept up a humorless banter which was about as appealing as a sopping wet bedroll. To pass the time, Fargo looked about at the audience, noting the spiffed-up citizens of Cedar City sitting alongside the fresh-scrubbed ranchers' wives in their homespun. When Frederico finished, they applauded politely. Then Magnus returned, wearing a yellow brocade vest and a red satin cape, leading Arabella, who had changed into a flowing green gown, low-cut and covered with silver stars and planets. The gaslights dimmed as Magnus helped Arabella onto a tall, carved throne which had been brought onstage. With a flourish Magnus blindfolded her and plugged her ears with cotton.

"Please notice that she cannot see or hear anything,"

Magnus said as he strode to center stage. "And now, esteemed ladies and gentlemen—the grand finale! I would not want to leave you with the terrible memory of the tragedy which almost happened this afternoon." Magnus paused and shuddered visibly. "No, my friends, now we will perform for you the most extraordinary feat of human endeavors . . . the reading of the human mind! Yes! The beautiful Arabella was born with the remarkable gift of mind-reading. And now, all I need is a volunteer from the audience."

Magnus stepped up to the gaslights and peered out toward the audience. He searched the faces and then locked eyes with Fargo.

"You, sir. No, you. There with the beard. Please come onstage."

Fargo got to his feet with a grin. This should be fun. The secret of this trick was probably a simple one, he thought. Magnus would ask him questions and Arabella could probably hear the answers because the cotton stuck in her ears was fake. Well, he'd just give false answers, he decided. And then see what would happen. Fargo leaped up onto the stage and Magnus shook his hand, his protuberant black eyes smiling. Magnus opened his mouth to speak, but Arabella's voice interrupted. Her voice was odd and seemed to come from all around them and, at the same moment, from very far away.

"There is no need to ask him questions," Arabella cut in. "I can read this man's mind very easily. He is an open book. Since I cannot hear you, touch my hand when you want me to begin."

"She already knows it is a man, even though she is blindfolded," Magnus pointed out to the audience. He turned to Fargo. "We have never met before, have we?" Magnus asked pointedly.

"Never," Fargo said.

"Fine. When Arabella speaks, you will shake your head yes if she speaks the truth and no if she is wrong." Magnus advanced to the throne and touched Arabella's arm.

"This man is a wanderer," Arabella began.

Fargo nodded. Most men were, he thought.

"He rides alone."

That too could be said of a lot of men, he thought as he nodded again.

"He is looking for a job now."

Fargo smiled. She was good.

"And a woman. He is always looking for a woman. Preferably several women."

Fargo laughed as did most of the audience. A few well-dressed matrons got up and left in a huff.

"He rides a black and white horse and he is very famous."

"Is that true?" Magnus asked Fargo, his voice edged with amazement.

"Yeah, I guess," Fargo said with a modest shrug, wondering how she had found out who he was. Arabella paused and raised her head as if listening to the voices of the mysterious beyond.

"His name . . . is Skye Fargo," she said. The audience murmured as people recognized his name. "And in his right jacket pocket you will find a purple handkerchief."

"She got the name right, but there's no—" Fargo reached into his pocket to turn it inside out and felt something inside. He pulled out a purple handkerchief. Fargo laughed with astonishment as the audience applauded. When had they slipped it in his pocket? he wondered.

Arabella removed her blindfold and came forward, grasping Fargo's hand and pulling him toward the footlights. She and Magnus took a bow as the audience cheered. Fargo squeezed her hand and she glanced toward him.

"What are you doing after the show?" Fargo asked her above the noise. "Can I take you to dinner?"

"That would be lovely," she said with a smile, her dark eyes dancing with light. "Come to the stage door."

Fargo moved off the stage as Magnus the Magnificent and Arabella took several more bows, and then the curtain rang down. The buzzing audience got up to leave.

Outside, the clapboard buildings of Cedar City baked in the July afternoon sun. Fargo rounded the brick theater and found the stage door in the alley. A burly man in a tweed cap positioned himself astride the open door. Inside, Fargo could see piles of crates and feathered costumes in heaps.

"Miss Arabella asked me to come see her," Fargo explained. The burly man eyed him suspiciously.

"Oh yeah? I've heard that story before."

Just then Arabella hurried by, dressed in the red-sequined costume.

"Oh, miss," the burly man called out. "This fella says you asked him to come see you."

Arabella stopped and stared at Fargo. The color rose in her cheeks and her dark eyes flashed.

"I certainly did not," she said. She moved away.

Fargo swore inwardly. Okay, if she didn't want to go to

dinner, she could have just said so. The burly man smirked.

"Move off, buddy."

As Fargo turned to go, the sound of angry voices drew his attention. They came from the other side of a brightly painted wagon standing at the far end of the alley. On the tall wooden sides of the wagon, in the midst of gold stars and comets, was written: MAGNUS THE MAGNIFICENT, THE WORLD'S GREATEST MAGICIAN. Underneath, in smaller letters had been added: WITH FREDERICO, THE FANTASTICAL CONJUROR. Fargo went to see what was going on. He rounded the wagon and then ducked back behind the corner, remaining just out of sight.

"You low-down cheating bastard!"

A bald mustached man had spoken. He stood holding a metal box firmly under one arm while Magnus was desperately trying to wrench it from him.

"I'm not cheating you!" Magnus said. "We agreed you'd get twenty-five percent."

"Well, it ain't enough now," the bald man replied, snatching the box out of the magician's grasp. "You're just trying to keep me down because you don't want us getting married."

"I pay you more than you deserve. Give me that money!" Magnus shouted, his face reddening with fury.

The bald man drew a short pistol and aimed it at the old man.

"You're crazy," Magnus said slowly, staring down the barrel of the bald man's pistol.

"I'm just tired of you not listening to me," the man said. "I been with this two-bit road show for a year now. And, I tell you, I want more than twenty-five percent."

"No," Magnus said. "What are you going to do? Shoot me?"

"Sure," the bald man said. "Some men came up the alley and tried to take your cash. Somebody shot you and I drove them off."

This had gone far enough, Fargo decided. He stepped out from behind the wagon, Colt in hand.

"Drop it," Fargo said.

The bald man whirled at the sound of his voice and instinctively pulled the trigger. The bullet sped through empty space as Fargo leaped to one side and then straight at the man, while holstering his Colt. Fargo hit him full force, knocking him into the dust. The cash box went flying. Fargo chopped the man's hand and he dropped his pistol as they rolled over and over, grappling. The bald man was surprisingly strong, his muscles like heavy iron bands. He drove his fist into Fargo's jaw, and the alley spun for a second. Fargo pulled back, shaking his head to clear it. Just then the bald man aimed another blow at Fargo's face, but Fargo brought up his left arm fast. The clout was deflected as Fargo brought his right back in and then sank a hard punch into the man's gut. The blow left him gaping like a fish on the ground, his green eyes furious. Fargo got to his feet and stood over the bald man, who finally groaned.

"You want more?" Fargo asked, covering the man with the Colt.

A furious look was his only answer.

"Should I let him up?" Fargo asked, directing the question at Magnus, who had retrieved the metal cash box. The magician nodded slowly, his eyes on the bald man, who got angrily to his feet.

"You're *nothing,* Frederico," Magnus said. Fargo looked again at the bald man and recognized him as the untalented conjuror in the show. Frederico looked a lot different without his silk turban. "*Nothing!* Got it? You're a lousy performer," Magnus continued, spitting out the words, his large eyes dark with anger. "No talent at all. I've tried to help you, teach you something about magic. And this is the thanks I get! You try to steal from me!"

"You . . . you just don't want me to marry your daughter," Frederico shot back.

So, Arabella was probably the magician's daughter, Fargo thought. And if she was engaged to Frederico, that explained why she wouldn't have dinner with him. But then why had she said yes in the first place?

"Shut up!" Magnus snapped. "And get out. Get your gear out of this wagon. I don't want to see your face again. Ever."

Frederico beat the dust out of his clothes and stomped toward the rear of the enclosed painted wagon. He jerked open the back door. Fargo glanced inside curiously. The wagon was half filled with stacks of colorful scenery, large mirrors, and other equipment that he couldn't identify. Frederico pulled several bags out of the back while Magnus watched.

"That one's mine," Magnus cut in. Frederico angrily slung a canvas bag back into the wagon and slammed the doors. Magnus stepped forward and padlocked them shut.

"Now, get out," he said to Frederico.

The bald man stalked down the alley while Magnus watched him go. Just then Arabella appeared at the stage door dressed in the green gown with silver planets. She glanced at the retreating Frederico with a worried look.

"Did you quarrel with him, Father?" she asked Magnus.

"I told him to get out," Magnus said. "And it's about time."

Arabella nodded thoughtfully. "So much for the wedding," she said softly, but without any emotion. Fargo wondered at her complete lack of feelings. Why had Arabella planned to marry Frederico if she hadn't even cared for him? Her gaze shifted and she seemed to notice him for the first time.

"Mr. Fargo!" she said. "I thought maybe you'd forgotten. Are you still interested in dinner?"

Fargo was completely confused. She was as changeable as a cloud on a breezy day. "Sure," he said doubtfully.

"I'll change my clothes. Be back in just a moment," Arabella said.

"Ahem," the magician said as he inspected Fargo. "So, you are taking my daughter to dinner."

"That's right," Fargo said with a smile. "Any objections?"

The magician's face wrinkled in a smile.

"I've heard of your reputation. You're the one they call the Trailsman. Honest man." Magnus's face darkened. "But likes women."

"Well," Fargo said, "I'm honest with women too."

Magnus smiled slowly. "Arabella is a grown woman. She will be fine with you," he said with a twinkle.

Just then she appeared at the stage door wearing the

red-sequined suit again. Fargo wondered if she meant to wear it to dinner.

"What have you done?" she shouted, running toward Magnus. She reached out as if to scratch her father as he caught her arms. She collapsed, sobbing, against the old man.

"He wasn't worthy of you," Magnus said, patting her shoulder. "Forget him. Forget him. There'll be other men. Much better men."

Fargo was just beginning to wonder if Arabella was stark raving mad when he heard her voice behind him.

"I'm ready!"

She stood at the stage door, decked out in a red-and-white striped dress with a matching parasol. The dress was cut low to show the curves of her breasts. Fargo stared at Arabella and back at the sobbing woman in Magnus's arms. The two women—twins, obviously—were as alike as two needles in a pin cushion.

"That's right," Arabella said, seeing the amazement on Fargo's face. She hooked her arm through his. "This is Adrienne, my twin sister."

Adrienne, hearing her name, looked up and wiped the tears away with the back of her hand. Magnus put his arm around her.

"My two girls," the magician said proudly. "They are wonderful on stage. And they come in very handy in many of our tricks."

Fargo remembered one of the tricks he had seen in the show, in which Arabella had been locked into a box onstage and made to disappear in a puff of smoke. Just an instant later—too fast for her to have gone through a trap-door and run under the theater beneath the audience—she had appeared at the back of the house. Now Fargo laughed as he realized how it had been done.

"Let's go," he said, touching his hat brim to Adrienne as he escorted Arabella down the alleyway and into the street.

"Get her home before midnight!" Magnus called after them.

"Not likely," Arabella whispered to Fargo.

As they swept up the boardwalk, Arabella's red and white dress and her curvaceous figure drew some appreciative glances from the other men. She didn't seem to notice but bent her attention entirely on Fargo as he told her about his work and his adventures on the trails of the West.

An hour later, they were seated in the dining room of the Cedar City Hotel. Fargo had just ordered roast beef, potatoes, and fresh asparagus and was refilling Arabella's glass with red burgundy when the waiter walked up.

"A telegram for you, sir," he said, handing a folded paper to Fargo.

He felt a rush of mild surprise. The only person who knew he was in Cedar City was old Colonel Parkin, a retired officer who lived north of town and whom Fargo had known years before in Kansas Territory. Fargo had visited the colonel several days before on his way into town to find another trail-blazing job. He opened the paper and glanced first at the name of the sender. The telegram was from Frank Giffin. A memory stirred in Fargo. He remembered Giffin. Sergeant Giffin, one of Parkin's best men.

"Trouble?" Arabella asked.

Fargo nodded absentmindedly and read the telegram.

FOUND YOUR WHEREABOUTS TODAY FROM THE COLONEL. NEED HELP. BAD TROUBLE HERE IN MIRAGE. LIFE OR DEATH. COME IF YOU CAN. FRANK GIFFIN.

"Yeah, it's trouble," Fargo said, tucking the telegram into his shirt. He called the waiter over and flipped him a gold eagle, asking him to send off a telegram to Mirage saying he'd be there in three days' time. After the waiter bustled off, Fargo sat back for a moment, his thoughts far away. He'd been through the town of Mirage once, a tiny settlement at the edge of the Hopi lands a hundred miles southeast of Cedar City. Strange country around there—colorful, empty desert with weird rock formations. Fargo shook off the memory as the dinner arrived.

All during the meal, Fargo successfully pushed away thoughts of Frank Giffin and the trouble in Mirage. Arabella was good company, he discovered. She had a ready laugh and a quick wit. They were waiting for the dessert and coffee to arrive when he remembered to ask her something that had been bothering him.

"So, how did you read my mind?" he asked with a wink.

Arabella dimpled. She picked up her dinner napkin and placed it on her head, holding it under her chin like a scarf.

"Excuse me, sir," she said in a cracked voice. Fargo started, then laughed, remembering the old blind woman in smoked glasses who had been begging in front of the Cedar City Theater before the show started. After he had dropped a half dollar in her tin cup, she stopped him and they had spoken for just a minute. From that brief conversation, he realized, the disguised Arabella had found out his name. The rest she might have known from his reputation, which had got around.

"How'd you know about my Ovaro?"

"Your horse?" she asked with a giggle. "I saw you tether it to a post before you came up to buy a ticket."

"I guess there's an explanation for every trick," Fargo laughed. "My favorite one was the floating—"

"The Wondrous Floating Woman," Arabella interjected.

"How did you do that one?" Fargo asked, remembering the astonishing sight of Arabella lying down, suspended in thin air six feet above the stage.

"Oh, no," Arabella said, suddenly serious. "That is one of my father's most famous tricks. There are a lot of other magicians who would like to get their hands on it."

"Like Frederico?"

Arabella's face darkened.

"He just wants money," she said. "And my sister. He's desperately in love with her."

"Did he ever bother you?" Fargo asked.

"Not since the first show I saw him do," Arabella said. "I laughed at him when he pulled a rabbit out of his hat and it made a mess down the front of his coat." She giggled at the memory. "I don't know what Adrienne sees in that man. Maybe she just feels sorry for him."

Fargo glanced toward the door of the dining room as he heard a loud voice. A familiar voice.

"Well, speak of the devil," Fargo said, looking over Arabella's shoulder. Frederico staggered in and stood swaying in the doorway. His collar was unbuttoned and his jacket on askew. His eyes were unfocused and he'd obviously been drinking. The bald man stared into the dining room, then spotted Fargo and Arabella. He headed for their table. The other patrons fell silent as they watched him weaving unsteadily through the tables.

"What the hell are you doing, stranger?" Frederico shouted. "You're going out with my girl!" A waiter hurried toward the intruder, but backed away when Frederico drew a knife from inside his jacket. As Frederico approached, Fargo stood slowly, all six feet of him, and Arabella turned around in her chair to look at the drunken man. Fargo noticed Arabella kept her wits about her.

"Get out of here, Frederico," Arabella said, her voice low but commanding.

"You heard what the lady said," Fargo added, resting his hand lightly on the butt of his pistol.

Frederico, seeing her face, backed away a few steps.

"Oh, it's you," he said, recognizing Arabella. The bald man shot a look of pure hatred at Fargo and sheathed his knife. He blinked a few times and held onto a nearby table for support. Then he turned and staggered out.

The dining room was abuzz with everyone asking who he was and what was going on. The feathered and fringed ladies of Cedar City craned their necks to stare at Arabella as they gossiped. Fargo heard the words *magic show* and knew she'd been recognized. Arabella seemed suddenly uncomfortable. The waiter appeared.

"Is everything all right here?" he asked. Fargo noticed that Arabella was squirming under the scrutiny and curiosity of the other diners. Somewhere quieter would be nice, he decided.

"Do you have private dining rooms?" Fargo asked the waiter.

"Yes. Several. There is one available right now."

"We'll take coffee there," Fargo said. Arabella shot him a look of gratitude, and he rose to escort her from the room.

The private dining room was hung in red velvet curtains and furnished with a small dining table, two chairs, and a large settee. Several fine paintings hung on the walls, and the oil lamps were turned low. As he held her chair, Arabella sank into it with a sigh of relief.

"This is much better," she said, looking around.

She was as pretty a woman as Fargo had ever seen, he thought as he looked down at her. The dark mass of ringlets fell over her smooth shoulders, and her black eyes shone with intelligence and humor. From this vantage point he looked down into her bodice and saw the swell of her breasts and the tunnel of cleavage between them. She looked up at him.

Fargo bent over her and kissed her lightly, exploring. Her hand came up behind his head and played with his ear lobe. Fargo nibbled at her lips, flicked his tongue delicately as he felt her open, taking his tongue deep into her mouth as if hungry for him.

The door opened and the waiter entered with a silver tray. Fargo straightened up as the waiter, his eyes downcast and pretending not to have seen them, approached the table. He poured coffee and set the slices of chocolate cake in front of them and beat a hasty retreat. As soon as the door shut behind him, Arabella giggled.

"I was waiting all night for you to do that," she said, a smile in her voice.

"Where were we?" Fargo said, bending over her again. This time he kissed her deeply, enjoying the fresh, sweet taste of her. She ran her hands over his strong back, and he felt her slender waist between his big hands. He moved one hand upward, cupping her full breast as she murmured in her throat.

"Oh, Skye," she whispered. "I've been hearing about you for years. And then, this afternoon, when I found out your name and . . . I hoped I would meet you. And I hoped . . . I hoped this would happen." Fargo stood and pulled her up out of her chair, holding her close, inhaling the perfume of her hair.

"I'm moving on tomorrow, Arabella," he said. "This telegram. There's trouble out near the Hopi lands. And I've got to go. You understand that?"

"I do," she said. She gazed up at him, her eyes serious. "But at least we have tonight."

Fargo kissed her again and she held nothing back, even grasping his hand and guiding him again toward her swelling breast. This time he slipped his hand inside the neckline of her low dress, and her breast overfilled his hand. He gently rubbed the warm nipple between two of his fingers and she moaned.

"Oh, yes," she said. "Let's."

Fargo moved away from her toward the door. He smiled to see that there was a brass lock on the door. Not enough to stop someone determined to get inside, but enough to deter a waiter and avoid an embarrassing situation. He threw the bolt and turned back toward her.

Arabella had moved to the settee. Her dress billowed around her, a huge cloud of red and white stripes. Fargo crossed the room and knelt on the carpet in front of her. He inched her dress up to her knee and bent to kiss her stockinged leg, flicking his tongue across the silk-clad flesh.

"You wicked man," she said with a laugh. Fargo kissed upward, circling her knee and proceeding up her thigh. She pulled her dress up higher about her, and his mouth reached her scented garters, the tops of her stockings, and then he was kissing the bare flesh of her thighs. The warm, musky odor among the lace made him feel suddenly drunk with desire. He hardened with wanting.

"You're going to love this," he murmured.

"I know," she sighed, resting back on the settee.